AF207173

Image
of
Deception

By Betty Briggs

Sunrise Selections

Copyright © 2000 by Betty Briggs

Photography by Scott and Betty Briggs
Graphic Design by Scott Briggs

All rights reserved. No part of this publication may be reproduced in any form without permission in writing from the author, except for brief quotations in a review. Additional copies are available from Sunrise Selections.

ISBN 0-9656307-2-2

Sunrise Selections
P. O. Box 51602
Provo, Utah 84605-1602

To my family of in-laws who make me proud to be a Briggs and continually treat me as if I've always been one.

Renewed thanks to my husband, Scott, for sharing his phenomenal computer and photographic talents.

Special thanks to models Ryan Bunker, Jared Bunker, Tressa Johnson and Bill Briggs and to horsewoman, Shelly Johnson, owner of Bandit (Midnight's stunt double). I acknowledge here my horse, Midnight, who will always be my good buddy and main equine model even though, born without a navicular bone in his front left hoof, he can never be ridden.

Thanks also to great writer friends: Rebecca Crandell, Linda Orvis, Lisa Peck, John Thornton and Milt Briggs for their patience and creativity.

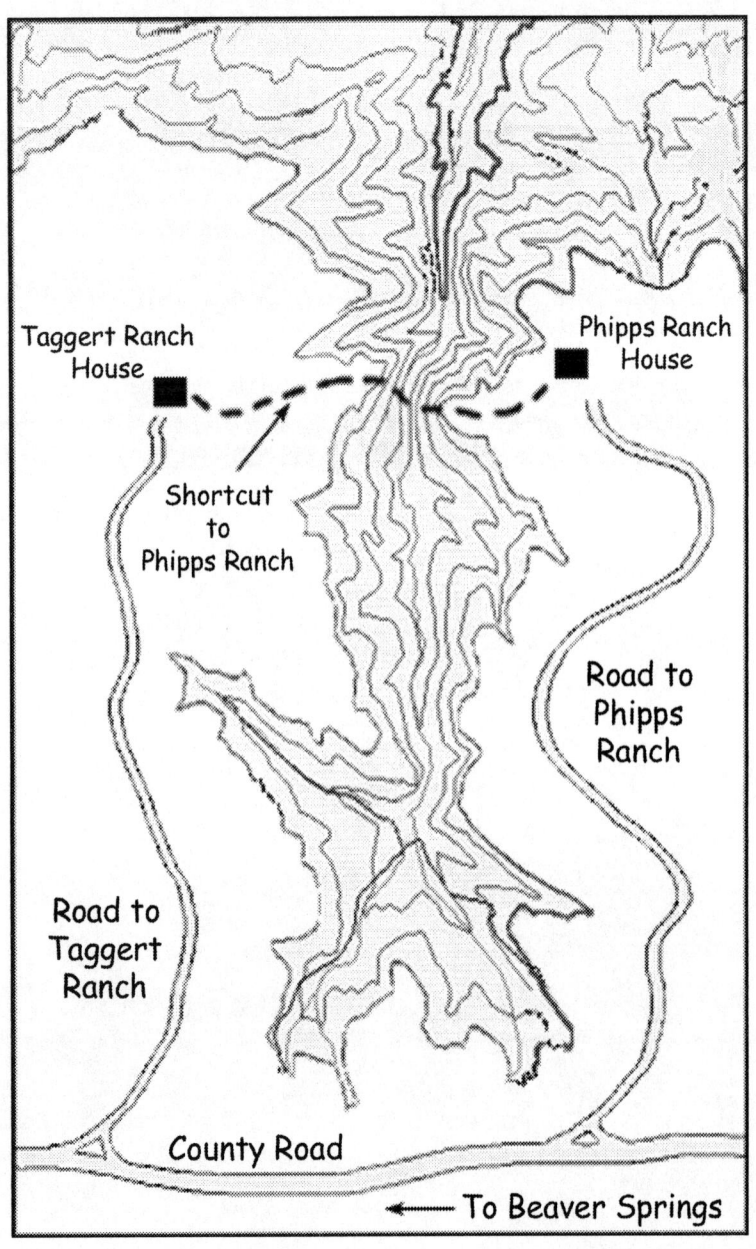

CHAPTER ONE

Heather Chambers stared at the stain on the faded front room carpet. She pressed a hand to her damp brow as the pounding in her ears magnified. *Stop it! Think about something else—David, Possum, anything.* She would not faint.

"That's where he did it. That's where old Charlie Phipps blew his brains out. Uncle Dallas helped clean up the mess." Katrina Taggert clung to Heather's arm as they inched farther into the old, abandoned ranch house. Her voice dropped to a whisper. "And now . . . now Charlie's come back."

Heather gulped a breath of heavy, stale air. "But he's dead now, you said, for over twenty years."

"That would explain the ghost."

"Ghost?" The static in Heather's head cleared. She shivered.

"I saw him standing right there last Thursday night." Katrina pointed with an unsteady hand.

"Come on. Don't make jokes about things like that, especially not here." Heather narrowed her eyes, blinked several times, and focused on the weather-stained window, the dusty threadbare curtains. "Couldn't it have been someone else?" She rubbed the back of her neck. What on earth was she doing here? She was a city girl from Utah, for Pete's sake, not some Montana ghostbuster.

Wagging a finger, Katrina said, "This isn't exactly Grand Central Station. I'll bet only a handful of people know about this place. And those who do remember probably wouldn't consider coming around—suicide and all."

"We should take a lesson from them." Heather walked wide around the brownish-red stain on the carpet.

Katrina touched the back of the lumpy, orange sofa then jerked away, brushing her hands together. "He came back, I tell you, to chase my family off his land."

Heather surveyed the room, the potbellied stove, the tin bucket filled with black chunks of coal. Except for an overall washed out, dusty appearance, the Phipps' front room probably looked much the same as when Charlie's wife left. "Why do you think it was Charlie? Do you know what he looked like?"

"I saw a snapshot—a black and white picture that fell from Mom's old purse when we cleaned out the closet. It showed Charlie, his wife Diana, Dad and Uncle Dallas, years ago when they were still friends."

Heather's foot slipped on something. She picked up an old issue of *Vogue*, dated May 1978, and thumbed through its pages. "I feel sorry for her."

"Who? Mrs. Phipps? How could you?" Katrina asked. "She knew how much Dad wanted this place. She had no use for it, but she wouldn't sell it, no siree." Her voice rose several notes.

"But look." Heather displayed the magazine. "Can't you see her sitting over there in that ugly, beat-up chair, dreaming of the things she read about—things she'd never have living way out here. But she stayed with Charlie and tried to make the best of it because she loved him." She sighed and batted her long lashes. "Then he killed himself . . . How awful!" She tossed the magazine aside. A puff of dust rose when it hit the floor.

Katrina coughed. "Yeah, yeah. Before you get all choked up, I hear there was another man in her life. I'll bet she told Charlie to get lost and that's why he did it. She probably felt guilty. That's gotta be why she blamed Dad and Dallas for her husband's death." She shook her head. "They tried to help him, even gave him a job on our other ranch. It was only after they caught him stealing calves that they fired him, that and he sopped up enough whiskey to float Texas."

Following Heather around the room, Katrina continued, "See these curtains? They weren't cheap back then, neither was the woodwork and the wallpaper. This was a pretty nice house when Charlie's parents lived here. I hear, in his dating days, Charlie wasn't too bad to look at and he could tell a good joke. The ladies hung around him. Uncle Dallas said Mrs. Phipps—he called her Diana—was real pretty. I think she drove Charlie to drink, always wanting more fancy stuff." Katrina flung her arms wide. "I'll bet she didn't even help her husband take care of what they had."

Somehow the vision of a cold and calculating Diana Phipps refused to gel in Heather's mind. It didn't matter anyway. She walked past the stove to a painting hanging on the soiled wallpaper. The man in the picture, riding a stocky buckskin, was especially well done and Heather wondered about the artist. Here too, she decided, Mrs. Phipps had tried to add beauty to her run-down surroundings.

"You know," Heather said, ducking to avoid a cobweb, "with some work, this house could be lived in again."

Katrina stared out the window, her hands alternately forming fists then relaxing. "The other night Charlie must have been standing right here."

Heather heard a rustle in the adjoining room. Was someone creeping across the floor? She held her breath. Something beat against the wall—once, twice, over and over.

Her hand flew across her mouth. She fought the instinct to run. Katrina seemed frozen in place. What gave Heather the courage, she would never know. She stepped toward the next room.

"You're not going in there, are you?" Katrina whispered.

Bringing her finger to her lips, Heather peeked through the door, her curiosity temporarily outweighing better judgment.

She laughed—a deep, rolling, relieved laugh. "Here's your ghost."

Clinging to the windowsill, a black and white magpie flapped its wings for balance.

Katrina collapsed against the wall, flung her hand to her heart and gasped. "That's it. I'm leaving," she declared, her blue eyes pools of determination, "and if you have the sense of an earwig, you'll do the same."

"What about the bird?"

"The bird?"

"He'll die in here."

"Let him get out the way he got in. I have no sympathy for something that scared ten pounds off me." Katrina rolled her eyes. "I can't afford that, you know."

Additional weight might have given the tall, skinny redhead some hint of a figure. Except for her height, Katrina looked much younger than her fifteen years.

"It'll only take a second," Heather said.

The June sun had started its descent toward the mountaintops. No way would she get caught anywhere near this house after dark. Even now she tried to shake off the feeling of being watched.

Katrina paced—faster and faster.

Heather struggled with the rickety window and looked for something to prop it open. A piece of old chimney pipe, lying in the corner, worked nicely.

Examining a splinter in her finger, she wondered what had become of Katrina. A blood-curdling scream came from outside. Heather bolted through the front room, tripped over a rug and caught herself against the stove. Two leaps and a scramble brought her to the porch.

Katrina, her leg lodged snugly in the shattered boards, trembled like a rat in a trap. "Help me! Help, Heather!" She jerked frantically on her unyielding leg.

"You scared me to death . . . careful." Heather bent to pry her new friend free. "Are you okay?

"Let's get out of here," Katrina wailed. "Charlie's around. I feel him."

Heather let herself be dragged to the waiting horses. Glancing at the upstairs window, she mounted her black gelding, who had already started off after Katrina's Palomino.

A curtain stirred. Probably the breeze.

But no wind fluttered the tiniest leaves on the cottonwood trees guarding three sides of the gray-toned house, or moved even one blade of tall, wispy grass at its chipped foundation.

CHAPTER TWO

Within the safety of the old Taggert barn, Heather brushed Royal Image until his black coat glistened.

The gelding pawed the freshly scattered straw on the floor of his stall. The scent reminded Heather of the stable back home and longing filled her heart, not for things as they were now, but as they had once been. She also missed her horse, Possum.

Turning her head from side to side, she tried to relieve the stiffness in her neck. At least at home she didn't have to worry about ghosts. What an experience. If only she hadn't glanced at that window as they left Charlie's house.

"So, Katrina." Heather hoped to make her voice sound light. "You said it was last Thursday that you . . . you . . ."

". . . saw Charlie's ghost standing at the window?" Katrina turned her Palomino horse into the stall next to Image. Normally Partner ran free in a huge pasture with the other ranch horses. Tonight he kept Image company.

"Or someone looking like Charlie."

Katrina sighed. "I thought we went over this."

Without warning, Image bared his teeth and lunged at Partner.

"That's gratitude for you." Heather tied the gelding's lead rope shorter. "Settle down, boy."

"I guess that's how it is with celebrities." Katrina's arms rested along Image's stall door.

"He just thinks he's special." Heather continued brushing the tall horse. "Was it the downstairs window?"

"What?"

"Where you saw Charlie."

"Yeah. I showed you, remember?" Katrina watched Heather silently for several minutes before continuing. "You're going to take the hide right off that horse if you're not careful."

Heather stopped, studied the brush, then dropped it into her tack box. "So what else happened? Tell me about seeing him." Picking up a blanket that lay folded on the straw beside her, she tossed it over Image's thin Thoroughbred skin.

Katrina smiled wide, displaying a mouthful of braces. "It was last Thursday afternoon, not long after we arrived at the Buck Place."

"This place, right?"

"Uh huh."

"So you have three ranches?"

"Yeah. Charlie's—the Lazy 6, this one—the Buck Place, and the home ranch. You do remember driving up from there this morning—the one that's seventy-five winding miles from here."

"I remember." Heather swayed back and forth holding her stomach. "I'm sorry you and your mom had to drive clear back to get me. I bet Kevin would have dropped me here." The way things had been going, he'd have probably done so gladly, to be rid of her.

"Actually it worked out great," Katrina said. "We needed to pick up more horses and some other stuff too. This is the first summer we've stayed here full time, and that's only because Dad was finally able to buy Charlie's land. It's got water."

What did water have to do with anything? She'd ask about that later. "I interrupted. Go on," Heather said. "You'd just arrived at the Buck Place and . . ."

"And . . . oh yeah, everybody was unpacking and stuff. I got so anxious I couldn't stand it. At the home ranch the night before, we finally got Dad talking about Charlie and the Lazy 6. He doesn't do that often." Katrina cocked her head. "I guess our finally owning the Lazy 6 and coming up here must have set him off. He mentioned things I'd never heard before, not even from Uncle Dallas, who's usually the only person to talk about Charlie. Dad doesn't say much about his old neighbor and if anyone else does, he changes the subject."

After securing the straps on Image's blanket, Heather selected a hoof pick from her tack box and lifted his front foot. "Your folks and Charlie were neighbors?"

"Uh huh. Years and years ago—when Dad thought he could work this ranch, before water got to be a problem."

"Hmm." Water again.

"I didn't know exactly how to get to Charlie's, only that there was a shortcut Uncle Dallas told me about . . ." She stopped talking until Heather looked up at her and straightened, dropping Image's hoof.

"I'm listening. That was one long shortcut." Heather patted her bottom.

Fresh in her mind and even more pronounced on her posterior was the memory of their hour-long ride zigzagging through sagebrush, pines and boulders.

"There's a mountain peninsula between the Buck Place and Charlie's Ranch." Katrina twisted her braid around her fingers.

"It's thirty-five miles of dirt road around the end of the peninsula between our house and Charlie's. The shortcut runs across that dividing ridge, but as you found out, it's narrow and rugged. A vehicle wouldn't make it."

"Did I leave the Absorbine out there?"

"Is this it?" Katrina retrieved the bottle of horse liniment and passed it across the stall door. "Do you want to hear the story or not?"

Actually, Heather wasn't sure. Was she afraid that learning more about Charlie would convince her Katrina was right? Had Charlie come back? Yes. Maybe. Of course not.

"Sure. Go on. I promise I won't interrupt again." Heather rubbed Image's legs.

"Okay. Where was I, oh . . . well, it took longer than I expected and it got pretty dark. I was thinking about turning back when something caught my eye." She paused and scratched the side of her nose. "A light . . . There was a light standing out against the dusk. When I got close, I could make out the outline of Charlie's house. I just sat there staring. The light came from the window I showed you."

"The window in the front room?" Heather asked.

"Yep. Partner snorted and I tell you, the hair on the back of my neck must have stood straight. Someone who looked exactly like the man in the photo stood there staring out. Partner whirled around. I gave him his head and on the parts of the trail that he could, he cantered home."

Katrina cleared her throat before continuing. "When we got here, Partner was dripping with sweat. Dad chewed on me for that, and for sneaking off by myself, returning after dark. I figured I was in enough trouble already, so what with him and even Mom always acting so peculiar about Charlie, I didn't tell him where I'd been or what I'd seen. Actually, I haven't told anybody except you. Fact is, I've been known to stretch a story now and again, so I was afraid no one would believe me. But, you do, don't you? Please say you do."

Heather thought of the night before at the home ranch, when she'd first met Katrina, buried in a book entitled *Mysterious Visits from the Beyond*. Somehow she could picture this girl with the long red braids, huge blue eyes and a sprinkling of freckles across her nose exaggerating now and again.

"I'll say one thing," Heather answered. "If there was ever a house that could be haunted, that's the one."

From out of nowhere a rope sailed through the air and settled around Katrina's shoulders.

In shocked silence, Heather, still stooping, watched for her friend's reaction so she would know what her own should be. What happened next took her by complete surprise.

"Ty," Katrina bellowed, "if you don't quit doing that, I'm going to cut out your heart and feed it to the coyotes."

Heather rose swiftly, coming face to face with a guy wearing a large cowboy hat and a broad grin.

Katrina untangled herself from the rope. "Heather, this is one of my big brothers, Tyler Taggert. He's seventeen, like you. He takes some getting used to, but you'll like him once you get to know him—unlike Colton. Actually, you'll probably like him too. Girls do. I can't see why myself."

Offering her hand then remembering it was still damp from horse liniment, Heather first wiped her palm on her riding pants.

He grinned again, peering out from under his big western hat. His eyes were root beer brown—like a cocker spaniel's. He'd probably be quite handsome when he filled out.

"Who's the sissy in the blanket?" he asked.

Before Heather could answer, Katrina spoke. "He's an expensive show horse and you're to treat him with respect." She delivered a punch to her brother's flat stomach.

"No kidding?" The boy vaulted over the stall door and came to rest beside Image, who jumped, knocked Heather's arm and splattered Absorbine down the front of her shirt.

"Did he hurt his leg?" Ty asked.

Heather flashed a nervous grin and screwed the lid back on the liniment. "No, he's just . . . well, like you say, a sissy."

Rubbing Image's neck, Ty said, "he's a good-looking sissy anyway. May I?" He began to unbuckle Image's blanket.

Heather stepped back. "Be my guest."

"Very nice," he said. "Good legs, long, well-balanced neck, and look at those shoulders. Reminds me of the mare I want to buy, only she's Quarter Horse. He's Thoroughbred, isn't he? Ever raced him?"

"He's a champion jumper," Katrina volunteered.

"Jumper, yes; champion, maybe someday," Heather added, "but he's got a lot of bad habits to get rid of first."

"That's why she's here. Her father . . ." Katrina said.

"Stepfather," Heather corrected.

She nodded. "Her stepfather is an old friend of Dad's. He used to ride on the U.S. Equestrian Team, but now he and Heather train jumpers. They bought Image last September at the Utah State Fair. He'd just tossed his rider in the show ring."

Had it really been the first of September, less than a year ago, since Kevin had rescued Image from his cruel owners? Along with Possum's win that day, then learning that Kevin and her mother were very soon to be married, Heather had felt her life couldn't be better. How could she have known then that the two people she loved most would reject her at the birth of their son?

Heather rubbed her forehead with the back of her hand. The scent of Absorbine made her nose twitch. Born two months early, Robby had only weighed four pounds, but even after her folks brought him home from a month-long stay in the hospital, they'd continued to shut her out. Her mom would hardly let Heather touch the baby, and no way could she tend him. At least that's how it seemed.

With Image's leg wraps in place, Heather offered the big black his ration of grain for the day and noted how Kevin's discriminating care had begun to cover the gelding's protruding ribs and hip bones with a slight layer of fat.

Ty replaced the blanket. "Tossed his rider in the show ring? I take it he's a bit playful."

"You got that right," returned Heather. "He picked up a lot of bad habits before Kevin bought him. They used to beat this horse." She shrugged. "Actually I've considered beating him myself. He can be a real dipwad. If we didn't believe he had so much potential, we'd have given up long ago."

Heather paused. Standing there grinning beneath that big, straw cowboy hat, Ty actually listened to her, not at all like David, who hadn't seen fit to even write after transferring to that fancy college back East.

Katrina passed Ty a healthy portion of hay and he dropped it into Image's manger.

Smiling her thanks, Heather continued. "Kevin felt that some ranch work might help—sort of clear Image's mind after all the training. I guess you could say we've about reached the end of our rope." She nodded toward Ty's rope discarded on the floor. All three laughed.

"Dang," Ty said. He lifted his hat to scratch his head. "I was sent out here to fetch you two for dinner. I guess we're all in for it now. Where ya been anyway?"

Heather hadn't noticed it before—well, how could she have with that huge hat, but Ty had tons of hair—thick, wavy dark locks, about the same color as Image. She wondered if the highlights of Ty's hair shone copper in the sunlight like they did on her horse. Ty really was cute, she decided, in a big kid sort of way.

"Just riding," Katrina said. Her look warned Heather against saying more.

Untying Image, Heather moved toward the stall door. Ty reached beyond her to open it. The door, on rusted hinges, screeched to a halt, but Ty didn't and Heather found herself pinned between his lanky frame and the door, complete with slivers.

"Dufus!" Katrina grumbled. She jerked the door open to free Heather, while glaring at her brother.

If the boy blushed, Heather didn't notice, for she was too busy feeling embarrassed herself.

Fortunately, a question she'd been meaning to ask popped into her head. "You said Image reminded you of a mare you've been looking at. Are you getting a new horse?"

Ty pushed his hat back on his head. "What an animal! You ought to see her. She's got a bloodline long as your arm." He frowned. "Of course Dad says I can't ride her papers so she's not worth all that money, but if I can swing it, I'm going to buy her and get some blooded horses on this place." His brown eyes glowed.

"My brother, the big talker." Katrina looped her arm through Ty's. "Dad's right, you know. You've got your hands full with all your horses and then there're the ones you're breaking for Dan and Gus. What do you want with another one, especially a mare that costs $2,500?"

Heather turned to face Katrina and Ty. "That's not bad, Katrina, really it isn't. Kevin pays far more than that for most of his horses."

"Katrina?" Ty said. "Just call her Katie, Kat, catnip, whatever."

"Katie's fine," she said, pulling a face at her brother.

They walked from the barn.

"Don't encourage him about the horse, Heather." Katie dropped her arm from Ty's. "He gets his mind set and that's all we hear about for years and years."

"Look who's talking." Ty caught Katie's braid. "It was your hounding about that house where Phipps killed himself that roweled Dad. He's real funny about it now."

Katie lifted a shoulder then backed away. Brother and sister stalked around each other like two dogs preparing for battle, but Heather noted grins teasing their lips.

It promised to be an eventful summer. Lots more fun than staying home where she wasn't wanted, and where she continually waited for some word from David. Being away when he got back from college for the summer would show she wasn't pining for him. She'd done that already. Now if she could just get Image whipped into shape before the state fair in September, maybe Kevin would remember she existed.

As they walked to the house for dinner, Katie stole a glance at Heather. Lifting her finger to her lips, Katie reminded Heather of the secret they now shared.

Heather nodded, though she wished she'd never heard the redhead's frightening stories or seen Charlie's old house, or . . .

She took solace in assuring herself she'd never go back, yet even then she knew it was a promise she could not keep.

CHAPTER
THREE

Katie toppled Ty's hat off his head and bolted for the house. He started after her, then stopped, plucked his hat from the ground, and picked up step with Heather.

At 9:00 p.m., sunlight still lingered in the vast Montana sky which stretched majestically from one rolling mountain range to another. Heather breathed deeply, rewarding her lungs with fresh, sweet air.

A dandelion-covered lawn and web-wire fence surrounded the aging, brick house into which Katie disappeared. Though the picket gate hung lopsided, Ty managed to open it for Heather without incident.

As they entered the house, he removed his faded Levi jacket and flung it toward a rack, full of coats and other wraps. Boots and boot overshoes, some covered with dried mud, lay piled beneath. Heather basked in the warmth of the room, wondering what to do next.

A bathroom lay off the large entrance hall where Ty splashed water on his hands and wiped most of the dirt on the towel.

"Want to wash the horse off your hands?" He offered Heather a clean towel.

She lathered up with pink, violet-scented soap shaped like a duck. Glancing in the mirror above the sink, she noted how limp and lifeless her long hair hung. Maybe her mom had been right about the whole hair-lightening deal. Heather guessed she really did look a little waifishly washed out—not at all like her seductive, naturally blonde friend, Sheila.

The last bit of water swirled down the old sink before Heather turned to search for Ty. She found him stooped in the hallway beside a cardboard box. A bulging gray cat peered up at the boy.

"Pregnant again, huh, Smoky?" He chuckled. "Did Mom let you in here, old girl?"

"What's that?" Mrs. Taggert walked into the hall.

Standing, Ty draped his arm around his mother's plump shoulder. He towered over her by almost a foot. "I was telling Smoky that she's one lucky critter, getting to stay in and all. Of course, I suppose at this time in her life, she needs her family around her." He winked at Heather.

No doubt about it. Ty enjoyed teasing his mother.

"I thought so too, dear," Mrs. Taggert said. She took Heather by the arm and led her into the kitchen.

"I should have been here helping you, Mrs. Taggert," Heather said. She'd met the woman the night before when she'd first arrived from Utah with her stepfather. Early this morning, she'd bid Kevin good-bye and driven up from the home ranch with Katie and Mrs. Taggert to join the rest of the Taggert family.

The bumpy ride in the two-ton Chevy truck, containing Image and several ranch horses, had been entertaining to say the least. Like Katie, Mrs. Taggert spouted juicy tidbits of information, but the similarity between mother and daughter ended there. Except for the fact that Mrs. Taggert was a shade on the chubby side, she more closely resembled her son. Ty had probably inherited his dark hair and friendly smile from her. Heather had liked the woman immediately.

"Just call me Bea," Beatrice Taggert told Heather. "Mrs. Taggert was my mother-in-law, long dead now, God rest her soul."

Smoky struggled out of her box and followed them into the kitchen, where she took up residency beneath Ty's chair.

An aroma of steak frying and fresh scones filled the room. Heather wondered how Bea had managed to prepare such a feast with so many other things to do.

The Taggert kitchen was far larger than Heather had supposed, and homey. Pots and pans with copper-colored bottoms hung on the walls above a wooden breadbox and ceramic cookie jar. Yellow curtains framed the window, accentuating a mountain peak in the sunset. The room was warm and cheery, made even more so by Bea's friendly smile.

"Sit here, dear." She offered Heather a seat between Katie and Ty. "Maybe it'll keep them from bickering."

"Me bicker?" An expression of innocence played upon Ty's face. Katie remained silent.

Heather took the offered chair and grinned her thanks to Bea who walked past Ty, sighed, tipped the covering off his head and hung the large hat on the rack.

"Boy, Heather," he said. "Are we ever in luck. I thought dinner would be long over by now and the dishes washed and put away. I guess Mom's slowing down these days." His brown eyes twinkled.

"Me slowing down?" Bea returned. "I wouldn't be talking about slowing down if I were you, young man. I'm just wise enough to allow time for dawdling when I send you on an errand. As a matter of fact, I thought you'd be longer. Your father and Colton are still washing up."

Heather had been so lost in the beauty and excitement of her surroundings and meeting Ty, that Katie and the adventure they'd shared had slipped from her immediate concern. But now, sitting next to her, Heather realized that her friend had been silent for a long time. Was she still thinking about this afternoon? Heather glanced at Katie and offered an unreturned smile. "Will you show me around after dinner?"

"Sure, unless you'd rather go with my brother." Katie took a quick sip of milk.

Heather guessed she had been a little too engrossed in Ty. At least Katie had quit worrying about Charlie, or had she?

"I'll bet she'd rather go with me," said a voice Heather failed to recognize.

She glanced up from the table and felt her mouth drop open. She hadn't meant to stare, but how could she help it? The voice came from the most gorgeous hunk of human she'd ever laid eyes on, at least since David left. And speaking of eyes, his were green, a green so electrifying they seemed to stand out like neon, or was it that his skin was so tanned?

It'd been a while since Heather had seen probably 190 pounds so spectacularly distributed over a six-foot-plus frame. From the top of his tawny brown hair, down to his stockinged feet, he was pure macho with a capital M. He reminded her a little of David. She sighed. This guy might be more handsome.

"Oh, no," Katie said. "Not you again."

"What happened, no plane to fly today?" Ty asked.

Good-natured kidding in this family had seemed to Heather as common as fleas to a hound dog, but Katie and Ty weren't smiling. Heather's glance darted from one boy to the other, then rested upon Katie.

"That's Colton," she whispered, "my stuck-up brother who thinks he's too good for us now that he's a big college sophomore. He's been taking flying lessons from Uncle Dallas in the ranch plane."

"I'm Colton," he said, holding out his hand. It seemed to Heather that he held on longer than for a normal handshake, but that was okay with her. She returned the smile, noting that in addition to his other admirable qualities, he had a very fine cleft in his chin.

"They told me you were coming," he continued, "but not how pretty you are."

Pretty? Heather had never considered herself pretty—cute perhaps. She felt she had the sex appeal of a freshly polished apple. Not long ago, David had made her feel special, but then he'd gone away to college and hadn't taken time to write, call or even e-mail. He'd probably found a blonde babe to occupy his time.

"Don't listen to him, Heather," Katie said, wrinkling her nose. "He's the world's biggest flirt."

Heather shrugged. So much for pretty.

In support of Katie's remark, Ty merely grunted.

"Okay guys, break it up," Bea said. "Where's your father, Colton?"

"Right here, my love." Wells Taggert sauntered into the room.

Glancing at him, Heather took a quick breath. Why did he look so familiar?

Wells dropped into a chair next to Colton. "Kinda reminds you of two bulls with their heads over the fence to the cow pasture, don't it, Bea?" He placed his worn felt hat on the table beside him.

Heather's face went hot.

"Wells!" Bea scolded, pushing a platter of steak toward him. "Here, eat your food." Then peering at his hat, she snatched it up, mumbling all the way to the rack

Back at the table, she spooned green beans onto her husband's plate.

"Old Kevin's a lucky guy, that's for sure," he said. "Is your mother as pretty as you, Heather?"

Good grief, like father, like son. "Mom's much prettier." She studied Wells, wishing she could place where she'd seen him before.

He was tall—not as tall as Colton, more Ty's height—and a little stocky. His belly hung over the top of his jeans a bit and caused the front of his plaid western shirt to gap open a trifle. Locks of sandy-colored hair, now streaked with gray, tumbled over his forehead, and every so often he'd reach up and coax them back into place. His mustache gave him a rugged, tough look, but smile wrinkles were etched around the eyes and mouth of his weather-beaten, yet handsome, face.

"Much prettier?" Wells chuckled. "Kevin always did like pretty women. We had a heck of a time that year in college. I guess I should've gone on and become a vet, but Dallas said they needed me on the ranch." He shrugged. "Oh well, I guess that's water over the bridge . . . a . . . under the bridge. Did Kevin ever tell you about the time we stole all those trout out of the fish hatchery and put them in the tubs at the girls' dorm?"

Heather hid a giggle behind her hand, then said, "I think he withheld that information."

"Wells! Honestly!" Bea said. "Heather will think we're heathens."

"Shoot, Bea," Wells grinned. "She ain't heard nothin' yet."

The dinner proceeded with only occasional distractions. Wells kept everyone, with the possible exception of Colton, entertained. Ty added flavor to the meal by sharing the experience of his horse, whose hoof, after stepping on a nail, swelled up like a five-gallon bucket. "I just soaked Black Jack's foot in a bunch of boiled sagebrush and you should have seen the maggots pour out. Rice, Kitty?"

This remark drew disapproving glances from everyone.

Then Ty's hand disappeared under the table one time too many.

"Tyler Taggert," his mother stormed. "I'll not have you feeding that cat at the table. It's bad enough she's in the house at all."

His grin widened. "She's not at the table, Mom. She's under it, see." He lifted the tablecloth and the water pitcher swayed.

Smoky began a hasty retreat.

Too late.

As Bea deposited the plump gray cat on the back porch, she said, "I'll save you some scraps, okay?"

Ty leaned over to Heather. "Two bits Smoky's back in before morning."

Bea returned to her seat with the dignity of a queen and the meal continued through dessert when Ty's plate slipped off onto his lap. Colton groaned. Katie giggled. Bea covered her eyes with her hands. Heather stifled a laugh.

Wells peered over the edge of his glass of milk and said calmly, "That's what you call an upside-down cake."

Until now, Heather hadn't noticed the strange designs around the edges of the plates and saucers. She figured this was as good a time as any to change the subject. "They're brands, aren't they?"

Ty lifted the plate from his lap, returning it to the table top. "That 'T' with the circle around it is ours," Katie pointed out.

"And this one's Slade Thompson's." Ty dropped the fallen chocolate cake back onto his plate. He nudged Heather. "He's the one with the mare."

Wells frowned. "Not that mare again, Ty. I've told you how silly it is to pay that much for a horse just because she's got papers."

"But Dad, you don't understand!"

"I understand more than you think. The subject's closed."

No one said anything for a moment. Although Heather agreed with Ty, she was relieved she'd kept quiet about the mare.

"That's a strange brand," she said finally, breaking the uneasy silence. "It looks like a six with a tail on it."

Katie choked on her water. Bea and Wells exchanged quick glances. Ty poked at his crumbled cake. Only Colton appeared unruffled. He leaned forward in his chair.

"If you look closely," he said, then stopped. "You have the most beautiful green eyes."

Katie groaned. Ty's nostrils flared.

Heat raced up Heather's face. "Thank you. I've always wanted blue eyes . . ." Quickly she thought about Ty, "or brown. Green seems boring, but your eyes are gorgeous."

Steady she told herself.

"Not as pretty as yours and sometimes mine change color." He pulled at the front of his green knit shirt. "Depends on what I'm wearing." He grinned. "As I was saying, Green Eyes, the top part of the six is a 'C'."

Heather had to tell herself to breathe.

"The bottom of the six plus the tail is a 'P,'" Colton continued. "That's old Charlie Phipps' brand. It used to be unpopular around here since it kept showing up on Taggert cattle."

Wells's palm hit the side of his plate, flipping his fork across the room with a clatter.

Katie shifted in her chair. Bea's hand shook when she handed her husband another fork.

Clearing his throat, Wells asked, "How's your flying coming, Colton? I hear you're going to try for your license soon." He shoveled in a mouthful of cake.

"Probably next week," Colton said. "Uncle Dallas has really been great. He's a terrific pilot, you know. We're going to fly to Salt Lake for more instruction, but I'll be ready soon."

"That's great, son. You've been spending quite a bit of time with Dallas, I guess?"

"He's been helping me a lot."

"I see."

"Why don't you just move in with him?" Katie asked. "We can't seem to get away from Uncle Dallas no matter what we do."

"That wasn't very nice, Katie," her mother said.

"But it's true. Isn't that why you and Dad are so anxious for this ranch to work out, so you can get away, not have him always interfering, sticking his nose into everything we do?"

"Kate. We have company," Wells said.

"You must be really smart to be a pilot at your age, Colton," Heather interjected. She pictured Colton in an airline pilot's uniform. Wow!

Tossing his crumpled napkin onto the table, Ty stood. "I'm going to bed."

Heather's eyes narrowed. What was his problem? Actually she knew. Lately, whenever her baby brother made an appearance, Kevin barely spoke to her. It seemed the same with Wells. He'd commented on Colton's flying, but allowed no discussion at all about the horse Ty wanted. Colton was awesome, no doubt about it. But Ty deserved attention too.

She didn't know yet, but later that night Ty would draw her attention—big time.

CHAPTER
FOUR

Image had no doubt worked himself into a lather by now, being in a strange place and all. Heather stood in the hallway between Katie's bedroom and the room which would be hers while visiting. Had it not been for her friend's ghost stories, Heather would have felt fine venturing into the dark to check on her horse. Remembering Katie's overactive imagination, Heather decided the girl's company would only make matters worse and Heather was too embarrassed to ask anyone else to go with her.

Angry at her trembling hands, she pulled on her jacket as she moved toward the mudroom just off the back porch. Was it her imagination or had something stirred behind her? She paused, straining her ears, and jumped when a voice said, "Tired of our company already?"

Heather took in a big breath of air.

"Well?" asked Colton.

"It's horse, my Image. I mean, it's Image, my horse," she stammered. "I have to make sure he hasn't kicked a hole in the barn or something."

Colton snatched a flashlight from a nearby shelf. "Would you like some company?"

"Why not?" Heather returned, trying to sound nonchalant.

As they were about to duck out the back door, Katie appeared. "Where ya going? To the barn? Wait a second, I'll go with you."

Heather noted the narrow-eyed stares between brother and sister and decided there was no love lost between these two.

"I guess we don't both need to go." Colton's hand brushed Heather's as he passed her the light. "See you tomorrow."

Katie trotted beside Heather on their way to the barn. "You're mad, aren't you?" the redhead said.

"Why should I be mad?" Heather's voice sounded harsh.

"I was only thinking of you."

"Me? How do you figure?"

Katie stared into the darkened surroundings and edged closer. "You'd get hurt. Colton's a war zone. He leaves scores of broken hearts wherever he goes."

Heather swallowed hard. Momentarily she'd flattered herself into thinking Colton could be interested in her.

"Do me a favor." Heather discovered she was more angry with herself than her companion. "Don't worry about me, okay? I can take care of myself." Sure she could. Since when? David was proof she needed pointers.

Suddenly Katie grabbed her arm. "Look!" she cried.

Heather turned where the flashlight cast its beam.

"There, don't you see it?" Directing her light once more, Heather watched as two brilliant beads of orange flickered like the eyes of a cat, yet she knew a cat's eyes didn't reflect that color.

"I wonder if ghosts' eyes shine orange," Katie gasped.

Ghost or not, it was downright creepy. "Tell you what," Heather whispered, "I'll race you to the barn."

Two breathless girls bolted through the door. Still running freely, Heather rammed into something solid. It moved. Strong arms caught her—wouldn't let go. She fumbled for the flashlight that slipped from her fingers. Her brow bone scraped against a hard, cold object—a button, a snap? A vision of the Phipps' cabin invaded her thoughts. Blood on the carpet. Someone at the window. Charlie! Her shriek pierced the silence of the night.

Image leaped against the side of his stall and blew through his nose.

A momentary thrashing of bodies ceased as the light blazed on. Heather blinked to clear her vision. Katie staggered from the light switch to a bale of hay and flopped down.

"Ty," Heather stammered. "I thought you'd gone to bed. What are you doing wandering around here in the dark?"

He rubbed his forehead with the tips of his fingers as if he too had experienced a shock. "Spooky little filly, aren't you?"

What must he think of her? His ears would probably ring forever. Heather felt stupid, no question, but there was something much worse to worry about. In her effort to escape the dangers of the night, she'd run directly into the boy, knocked off his hat and was at that very moment trampling it into the dirt floor.

"I couldn't sleep in there," he continued and peeked beneath her boots to what had once been his hat. "I was just about ready to bed down here with the horses."

Heather stepped aside, picked up his Stetson and tried to mold it back into shape. "I'm sorry." She passed it to Ty. "I guess I'll have to make this up to you."

"That's okay," Ty said, with a seductive lift of his brow, reminiscent of his brother. "Someday I might let you, but not just now."

"You guys are talking about hats when we pert-near scared ourselves silly?" Katie ambled toward the others. "I don't know what that bloodcurdling scream did for your systems, but it sped mine up considerable."

Heather shifted from one foot to the other.

"Why did you two come barreling in here like broncs out of a buckin' shoot?" Ty asked. "You'd think you'd seen a ghost or something."

Katie stared at the ground.

Heather walked toward Image. "You know how a cat's eyes shine in the dark?"

"You're afraid of cat eyes?" Ty followed closely.

"It couldn't have been a cat." Heather stopped in front of the horse's stall. "What we saw was bright orange."

The black gelding stomped.

"It was probably a fox then." Ty leaned on the stall door.

"A fox?" both girls echoed.

"Sure, fox eyes shine red or orange. Deer's shine green. You should've known that, Katie."

"Excuse me?" she replied. "I don't go around peeking into wild animals' eyes in the dark."

"Watch out!" Heather cried.

Teeth bared, Image acted as if he fully intended to finish his meal with a chunk of Ty's arm.

The boy placed his hand on Image's nose, giving it a firm shove. "Do you like this horse?"

Heather shrugged. "It's a struggle some days."

Ty checked the sturdiness of the stall door. "Why do you put up with him then?"

She'd had asked herself that question a million times lately. Image wasn't even her horse. He belonged to her new stepfather. Her own sweet, gentle horse, Possum, had carried her to victory in the Jumpers Stake last year at the fair. "It's a long story."

"He's good looking enough," Ty continued, "but I could help you find one a little less obnoxious. That mare I want has a half brother. Sound interesting?"

"No . . . I can't."

"Why not?"

Heather yearned to be free of Image, but he was the horse Kevin wanted, the horse in which he'd placed his faith. Her mouth twisted. "My stepfather likes him."

"He should ride him then."

"It's more than that. Let's see. How to begin? Kevin's had a rough time. Two years ago, he lost about everything. His daughter died in a jumping accident. His wife divorced him because she blamed him for Wendy's death. Horses reminded him so much of his daughter he couldn't stand to ride anymore. He quit the U.S. Equestrian Team and sold all his horses. Now, I guess you could say, he's rebuilding his life."

Opening Image's stall door, she walked in. He moved to the back, then turned to face her. She held out her hand and edged closer, touching his neck. He quivered.

Ty joined her at the gelding's side, taking hold of the halter.

"Being into horses yourself," Heather continued. "I imagine you know how it is when you love them so much and then they're not around anymore. You ache inside. Kevin thinks Image has potential. I want him to be right. He needs that confidence in himself again."

"And Kevin's so handsome," Katie added. She stood at the gate to Partner's stall, stroking the Palomino's nose.

"He is handsome." Heather smiled at the younger girl, then resumed her explanation. "Your ranch is sort of a last resort. Right after Kevin brought Image home," she rubbed her hand down his black neck, "he jumped so well. He started eating better and even put on a little weight. We entered him in some top shows in California. Then for some reason, he went sour, started crashing jumps and refusing. We tried everything. Kevin finally decided a change of scenery and complete rest from advanced training might help. That's when he called your dad."

Heather chewed her lip. More than anything, she wanted to please her stepfather. If she could get Image jumping again, surely Kevin would love her again, or at least pay her some attention, like he had before her new brother was born. She guessed she couldn't blame her stepdad. An adorable son like Robby was every man's dream.

"I'm glad you told me," Ty said, walking from the stall. He glanced at Heather.

Her eyes misted as she thought back to the good times she and Kevin had shared, on occasion with her mom—the evenings studying show jumping videos over popcorn. She remembered the horseback rides, the long talks, his wise counsel—always listening, never condemning—and his encouraging remarks. Kevin had almost succeeded in filling the emptiness the death of her real father had left.

"I'm sorry," Ty told Heather. She followed him out of the stall and he secured the door. He touched her shoulder. "I didn't mean to make you sad. Image is a good horse, really he is—a little pigheaded—but good just the same. I'll help you with him."

"He can, Heather, really," Katie added, stepping toward them. "He trains horses for most of the ranchers around the home ranch. He even won a silver buckle in the bronc riding at the Labor Day rodeo last year." She pulled up Ty's jacket. "See?"

Heather smiled and blinked back tears. "I could use some help. Thanks."

She turned to Katie. "Ready to go back?"

"You're coming too, aren't you, Ty?" Katie quickly asked.

Ty dropped his arm around Katie's shoulders. "Doesn't this sisterly love just choke you up?"

Katie stuck out her tongue.

"Good night, you ignorant old devil," Ty told the gelding.

Image snorted.

Ty and the girls walked out the door.

The trip back to the house seemed shorter with Ty along. As they entered, he nudged Heather. "What did I tell you?"

Smoky lay snuggled in the rags of the cardboard box, just as she had earlier that day. It didn't take much of an imagination to visualize a smile of contentment upon her whiskered face.

After sharing milk and cookies with Ty in the kitchen, Heather met Katie headed for her bedroom. "What's the world coming to?" Heather said, still thinking about Katie's intervention with Colton. "You actually left me alone with Ty?"

"With Ty," Katie said, yawning, "you don't need protecting."

It was like watching herself on film. Heather remembered this same thing happening before, but now she seemed strangely detached. Night hung close. She and Katie strolled to the barn, chatting about something. Then Katie said, "Oh, look. There's a fox. Do you see his bright orange eyes?" Heather turned. Her flashlight revealed the glowing glare, but no fox. A man ran toward them, carrying a long, narrow object. Closer now, he lifted his arm to strike. Heather screamed. Just before he swung at her, she realized what the man carried—a branding iron displaying the strange 6-with-a-tail symbol.

Heather screamed again. She was still surrounded by darkness, but the film had stopped. She felt hands on her shoulders, shaking her. Ty's voice. Light flooded the room and three concerned faces stared at her as she struggled to sit up.

Leaning close, Bea perched on the bed beside her. "What is it, dear?"

"Are you okay?" Katie asked, her blue eyes as wide as wagon wheels.

"You city girls sure do scream a lot." Clad only in a pair of jeans, Ty had apparently left his room without taking much time to dress. Heather had the fleeting impression that earlier his western shirt had surely hidden extremely broad shoulders and rippling muscles in his arms, chest and belly.

If she'd had been embarrassed in the barn earlier, it was only an inkling of what she experienced now. Humiliation heated her face to boiling.

"This isn't me." Heather massaged her brow with the tips of her fingers. "I can't remember the last time I acted like this."

"It was earlier this evening with the horses, remember?" Ty dodged her punch.

"I mean before that." Heather touched a palm to her cheek. "Honest, I don't know what's come over me."

Bea opened her mouth but said nothing. Someone stumbled down the hall.

"Ouch!" a voice said. Heather hoped it wasn't Colton. The situation bordered on grim already.

"Is it morning?" Wells stuck his head through the doorway.

Bea smoothed Heather's hair. "She had a nightmare."

"Oh good. If it was a nightmare, it must still be night. Come to bed, Bea." He started to leave, then turned back around. "Did something upset you, Heather?" He glanced at Katie who studied the floor.

"Oh, no. It's . . . oh, I don't know." She looked back and forth between father and daughter.

The man's eyes narrowed

Katie twisted her long braid around her finger.

"Come along Bea. And Ty, I believe your room is down the hall to the right."

For the rest of the night, Heather stared at the ceiling, tossed and turned, then stared at the ceiling some more. Whenever she'd close her eyes, that same horrible face with the ghastly, orange eyes appeared.

Only the first rays of morning sun had filtered in along the edges of the bedroom blinds when Heather dragged herself from under the covers. Since sleep proved impossible, she decided it was a perfect opportunity to give Image a workout without an audience.

Heather's head ached and her eyes burned. She pulled on a knit shirt and a pair of blue jeans and shuffled to the bathroom where she doused water on her face. Grabbing a jacket, she left the sleeping household and started for the barn.

The sun still rested upon a horizon of rolling mountaintops and cast a warm, pinkish glow on the dew-covered landscape. Heather's head cleared and again the excitement of the ranch possessed her. How could she have let a dream cause so much upset?

Image greeted her as he often did, with ears pinned against his neck. "Get a grip, will you?" She acted more confident than she felt. ". . . And not on my arm."

When Image's show of bad temper failed to produce a reaction, his ears changed direction and he sniffed her outstretched hand. Whiskers tickled her palm as he scooped up an alfalfa cube.

Katie had called him a champion jumper. If only that were true. It wasn't that he didn't have the ability. He could jump like a gazelle when he wanted to. Lately, though, they'd been unable to convince him that he wanted to.

Heather warmed the bit in her hands. Image raised his head and fought the bridle as she tried to slip the headstall over his ears. She stretched to her full five-foot three-inch height. Then on tiptoes, arms up, she completed the task. While Image tried to push the bit from his mouth with his tongue, she straightened his forelock.

Every so often, if only to keep from sending him to Purina for dog chow, Heather forced herself to remember last year at the fair, when she'd first seen the gelding. She could still picture the blood dripping from his lips as his rider jerked on the reins and the horse's fear-filled eyes when whipped over jumps. But that was in the past, and he still behaved like he'd never felt the touch of a gentle hand.

Before Kevin returned to Utah, he'd instructed Heather not to jump Image for a while. But if she set the jumps low enough, the gelding might go over them and she could get on with his training. How she'd love to surprise her stepfather.

Gathering discarded barrels, poles and the broken off tongue from an old manure spreader, Heather designed three jumps.

After a brief warmup, she directed Image toward the makeshift obstacles. Here there were no confines of the show ring or her practice course back home. At first the openness seemed to appeal to the gelding. He leaped all three willingly and Heather's spirits soared. Then she suggested he go in the opposite direction. He hurdled the first obstacle and cantered on to the next. Collecting himself in preparation for that jump, Image apparently changed his mind and stopped short in front of it. Heather saved herself from a hasty dismount by grabbing his mane.

Sweat trickled down her face. She kicked him around to the first jump. He refused again. Heather choked on the lump in her throat. Why hadn't she listened to Kevin? What on earth should she do now?

Every instinct in her body urged her to take Image back to the barn and forget the whole incident, but she knew she couldn't. Image had to learn to obey.

Heather gathered the reins in her hands and cantered the gelding in a tight circle for control. He fought for his head and changed leads. Seeing the jump ahead, he trembled. She trembled too. The jump loomed closer with each of Image's long strides. On impulse, she grabbed the horse's mane just as he crashed into the obstacle. He whirled and reared, striking out with his front hooves. She felt herself slipping and clawed for balance. As he rose higher in the air, she tumbled to the ground.

Pulling herself to a sitting position, she stared directly into the knees of someone's nicely fitted jeans. Slowly she scanned the trim body upward to Colton's sea green eyes. Gladly she'd have burrowed into the ground like a mole.

"If you'd get a regular saddle, you'd have better luck sticking to that bronc," he said.

Heather's black leather jumping saddle had no horn, unlike the western saddles used on the ranch.

She said nothing.

"Are you okay?" Colton continued. "Here, let me help you." Taking her hand, he pulled her to her feet. When she swayed, he put his arm around her shoulder.

A horse snorted and Heather saw Ty leading Image in their direction. She tried to think of something clever to say but managed only, "Don't you guys ever sleep?"

"Don't you?" Colton asked with a grin.

Ty handed Heather the bridle reins. "What did he do, dump you?" he asked. This was a harsher Ty than the one she'd shared cookies with the night before.

Moving out from under Colton's arm, Heather gazed up at the saddle.

"Want a boost?" he asked.

At first Heather just stared. Image grew impatient and sidestepped. "I can't do it," she said.

"You should, you know." Ty, voice gentler now, sounded more like his old self.

"Well, actually," Colton grumbled, "what difference does it make? She'd rather come with me to salt cattle, wouldn't you, Heather?" He moved closer.

"I don't know about the cattle, but I can't get back on right now."

"Let's go then." Colton reached for her arm.

Ty stepped between them. "It makes a lot of difference and she knows it."

His words cleared her head. She did know it. If Image kept giving her problems, Kevin would forbid her to show the horse. She hadn't even told her stepdad about some of Image's worst outbursts. Already he'd suggested the gelding might be too much horse for her and that he should take over the training. No way. If Kevin took her job, he wouldn't need her at all.

At the thought of losing Kevin's trust, tears filled Heather's eyes. What was wrong with her? She was acting like one of those drippy, sentimental females she so detested.

This time Ty came to her rescue.

"Listen, Heather, it's no big deal. I'll take him over the jumps if you want. Then he won't be getting away with anything."

She chewed her lip. Maybe Ty could get Image to jump. Although she felt like she'd lost all purpose to exist, she desperately needed a way out right now. Perhaps the horse would be easier to ride another day.

"Do you think you can?" Heather asked.

"My dear girl," Ty said, "you're looking at a man who breaks broncs for a living, rides Brahmas for pleasure and eats nails for breakfast."

Colton sighed and Heather laughed in spite of the tears rolling down her cheeks.

Adjusting the stirrups, Ty boarded Image before the horse had a chance to object. His long legs dangled at the gelding's sides. "Well, tallyho," he said, lifting his hat. With a pang of guilt, Heather noticed he wore a different one this morning.

Ty circled the black, then headed for the first fence. Image stopped momentarily, but Ty's powerful legs and firm, directing hands urged the horse onward. Image floundered over the first jump, crashed through the second, but cleared the last with inches to spare.

Bringing the gelding around to Heather and Colton, Ty said, "See, Heather, we can train him. Everything will be okay." He slid off Image and rubbed the horse's long, sleek neck. "He's a big bully, that's all."

Suddenly a sickening realization came over Heather, making her dizzy. She'd lost her nerve.

"Come on," Colton said. "Put the beast away and let's get going."

Heavy thoughts kept Heather from objecting or even commenting on Image's performance.

"I'll put him away." Ty turned and, without a backward glance, stormed off to the barn, leading the prancing gelding.

Mouth ajar, Heather watched them go. Was Ty upset about something?

Had she known where she and Colton were headed, she might have stayed behind even if it meant another battle with Image.

CHAPTER
SIX

Heather glanced across the seat of the four-wheel-drive pickup. Feeling an inner stirring of approval, she noted Colton's handsome profile—the straight line of his features, the strong jaw. Unlike his father and Ty, who dressed like cowboys, Colton wore regular work boots, Levis and a knit shirt the same deep green as his eyes. No hat hid his light brown hair, which hung just long enough at the back to brush the top of his collar. She fought the desire to bury her fingers in those tawny locks at the nape of his neck.

Instead her nails dug into the armrest. Never should she have allowed Ty to take over with Image. The next training session would be far worse than the one she'd ditched today. She dreaded it already. Some horsewoman.

"What?" Colton said.

Quickly she redirected her stare. "I was just thinking how . . . how gorgeous it is up here."

"It's pretty, all right," Colton returned, drumming his palms on the top of the steering wheel, "but that's about it. I can't tell you how anxious I am to get back to college. Uncle Dallas is the only one around here who understands I want more out of life than this."

Uncle Dallas again. Heather remembered how Wells had hung on Colton's every word the night before, much to the exclusion of Ty. Did Wells fear losing his older son to Dallas?

"That's where old Charlie Phipps committed suicide," Colton said.

Heather's mouth fell open, but no words came out. For hours she and Colton had driven through mountain rangeland replenishing salt licks, which Heather had learned were the large, trampled down circles in the grass that surrounded the pitted and distorted salt blocks from prior months. She'd been so disoriented she had no idea where their journey had led them. They must have traveled around the end of the mountain peninsula that she and Katie had crossed the day before on horseback.

"Sorry. I didn't mean to startle you." Colton brought the pickup to a stop for a better view. "I thought Katie might have told you the story."

"She did mention something. You caught me by surprise, that's all."

To Heather, the house looked much the same as it had the day before—creepy, but there was something else. From where she sat now, she could see a cluster of three outbuildings, one bordered by a high pole fence. Why hadn't she noticed them before? Oh, she saw why. Like the house when they were viewed from certain directions, trees and the rolling terrain camouflaged them.

"Killed himself? How awful!" Her response had been for Colton's benefit. She glanced at the upstairs window. Nothing moved.

"He's the man with the strange brand we talked about at dinner last night," Colton said.

"Yeah. I remember," Heather said, carrying on the charade.

Some cattle turned to watch them. A pure white cow wandered toward the truck.

"Phipps used to own all this land, but now it belongs to us," Colton said.

"That's what Katie said. She mentioned your ranch is more valuable now that you have Charlie's water. Why doesn't the Buck Place have water?"

"It did, twenty-five years ago, when my father bought it. He brought Mom here and started ranching on his own. I think he wanted to get away from Uncle Dallas." Colton shook his head. "I can't understand it. I've never had trouble getting along with my uncle. Sometimes he's easier to be with than Dad." He paused, his attention on the cow. "What's she doing?"

The animal made a wide circle around the truck.

"What kind of cologne are you wearing? She's female. Don't all the girls go for you?" Heather said.

"Was that a compliment?" His brow lifted.

"If you like cows." Heather grinned.

He licked his index finger and made an imaginary mark on the windshield. "That's one for the kid."

Still grinning, Heather asked, "So how long has your family owned the home ranch?"

"Oh, probably fifty years. My grandparents bought it, but they were killed in some kind of a farming accident when Dad was about eighteen. They left the home ranch to Dad and Uncle Dallas. Since Dallas is five years older he usually takes the lead in running things."

"Didn't he want your dad to buy the Buck Place?"

"No. They didn't need another ranch or the expense. I think Dad just wanted a place of his own." He shrugged. "Everything might have turned out okay had it not been for the earthquake."

"The earthquake?"

"Yeah. After that Dad's spring dried up. Charlie's got bigger. Lots of strange things happen to land after an earthquake. Dad tried to deal with Charlie for use of some of his water, but the jerk wouldn't even talk about it."

The cow had stopped walking, but her head still turned toward the pickup.

"Why didn't Wells just sell the Buck Place?"

"It would have been a huge loss. You can't have a going ranch without water. Since Dad had to give up some of his shares in the home ranch to pay for the Buck Place, we've just pastured it during the summers hoping something would give."

The cow nosed the truck, waking Jake, who started to bark. Jake was, as Colton put it, the best cow dog on the ranch—a fortunate fact since with his scarred face, crooked tail and piebald color, he'd win few beauty contests. Wherever this particular pickup went, Jake rode lookout.

"Dad's funny about this place," Colton said, watching the cow. "Uncle Dallas told me Dad wants to tear it down. Seems like a waste to me . . . Friendly old gal, isn't she? I wonder where her calf is?"

"What makes you think there's a calf?"

"That's what she's looking for. See that orange tag hanging from her ear? The color means she's four years old and the thirteen matches the number on her calf's ear tag, which this year would be blue. The cow would have a zero on her tag if she hadn't calved this year."

"Maybe it died," Heather offered.

"Maybe." He rubbed his chin. "Doubt it, though."

Heather sighed and studied Charlie's house. If she were ever to put her mind at rest, she'd better do it now. She'd take a quick peek. No way would she go upstairs. She'd just check out the front room and make sure the bird had escaped. "I've got this thing for old buildings. Do you mind if I take a look?" She nodded toward Charlie's.

"Suit yourself. Katie seems to think the place is haunted, but you know Katie."

Relieved she hadn't mentioned anything to Colton about the day before, Heather said, "I'll only be a minute."

"Take your time," he said. "I have to drop some blocks around those trees. We should be heading home soon, though, before Mom sends out a posse."

Heather reminded herself that she was within screaming distance of Colton as she walked toward the old house. Its windows glared at her, but its door beckoned her closer. The face in her dream flashed before her and she almost turned back. "You big chicken," she told herself and set her jaw.

"There's no such thing as a ghost. There's no such thing as a ghost," she said as she crept across the squeaky porch and through the front door. She began to breathe easier when she noted nothing had changed in the front room since yesterday. No sound of the magpie either.

As she turned to leave, she stopped short, looking from one wall to the other. Her stomach twisted. Not everything was as it had been. The cowboy picture that had so fascinated her the day before was missing. Something else gnawed at the back of her mind—something about the painting. She drew a quick breath. It couldn't be. Think back. Concentrate. Okay. Now she knew where she'd seen Wells Taggert before. He was the man in the picture.

Why hadn't Katie noticed the resemblance? Haw. She'd been so nervous she'd barely been able to focus on anything.

What was that? A sharp, clanking sound. It sounded like . . . couldn't be. There it was again. It sounded like a chain dragging across the floor in the next room—the magpie room. But this was no magpie!

The front porch squeaked and Heather's knees nearly buckled. Her heart thumping wildly in her chest, she poised for action.

"It's only me," Colton said, glancing back and forth.

"I heard something in there. It sounded like chains dragging," Heather blurted.

Colton chuckled. "I think you've been spending too much time with Katie." He walked to her and she grabbed his arm. "Come on, let's go see." He placed his hand over hers, which still clung to his arm and they headed to the next room.

No mysterious being lurked there. In fact everything looked exactly as it had the day before—even the chimney pipe.

"Are you satisfied, or would you prefer a more thorough investigation, Inspector?" Colton grinned.

Heather wasn't satisfied, but she felt so silly that she kept quiet. She wished she'd stayed in the truck. Things were worse than before. She knew what she'd heard—and the painting. Where was it?

"That's okay," she said. "We better go."

Heather realized she still held onto Colton's arm. Quickly she pulled away and backed up. He reached for her hand and drew her to him. Lowering his head, his lips touched hers.

She'd expected fireworks like when David kissed her. Not so. Of course, there was that little matter of Colton's other girlfriends, and the setting—not exactly the romantic atmosphere she'd have picked. She stiffened.

"What's wrong?" Colton leaned away to stare at her.

Heat prickled at the back of Heather's neck and she stammered, "Oh, nothing. Lack of practice, I guess." She bolted through the front room and out onto the porch, stopping only when she saw the white cow lingering between the cabin and the safety of the truck. The pickup looked a long way off—still parked beside the last salt lick, a pasture length away.

Colton joined her outside and they stepped off the porch. "I wish I'd parked closer," he said. "After I dropped off the salt, I thought I saw her calf. It was like one of those mirage deals when you keep walking toward something and it's always farther away than you think. Next thing I know, I'm right here by the cabin, staring at a mound of dirt."

Off to the side, several yards away, the cow lumbered along with them.

"She wasn't this interested in me earlier. Must be you she's after." Colton picked up a rock. "You know, cows are more dangerous than bulls when they charge. They keep their eyes open—bulls don't."

The cow turned in their direction.

"Where's Jake?" Heather asked.

When the cow started to trot, Colton flung the rock at her. It hit her alongside the head. Snot sprayed from her nose as she snorted. She came at them faster.

"Run!" he yelled.

The cabin looked miles away—so did the truck.

"Run where?" Heather cried and started off, her throat tight.

Colton trailed behind, the cow in hot pursuit.

"We won't make it," Heather squealed.

"Over there," Colton yelled, "the trees."

They set out for the grove of cottonwoods.

A branch nicked Heather's hand as she scurried onto a low hanging limb. She edged several branches higher. Colton caught the limb with both hands and swung up with ease. The cow stood beneath, pawing the ground.

Heather and Colton stared at each other, then burst out laughing.

"We'll have to make up another excuse for being late," he said. "No one will believe this."

"Look." Heather pointed. A ball of barking black and white darted nearer.

Jake leaped in the air and buried his teeth in the cow's nose. Furious, she tossed him to the ground. He jumped up and attacked her heels.

"Like I said before," Colton began, "Jake's the best cow dog on the ranch—when he isn't snoozing."

While Colton watched the battle, something else drew Heather's attention. From where she sat in the tree, she could see a structure near the cabin that from ground level would have been concealed behind grass and underbrush. It seemed to be a stairway leading into the earth.

A root cellar. That's what it looked like. Its front wall consisted of solid timbers with a door appearing elephant strong.

Meanwhile back at the battlefront, Jake had succeeded in drawing the cow away from the tree.

"Come on, now's our chance." Colton leaped from the tree, stopping only long enough to help Heather down.

Running for the pickup, Heather stumbled. Her hand broke her fall and plowed through the dirt. Something blue slipped over her fingers. Before struggling to her feet, she grabbed the object.

As Heather and Colton slid into the truck, she glanced down at her hand. A blue tag with the number thirteen clearly imprinted on it lay in her palm. "Looks like I've found the missing tag," she said. "I wonder where its calf is."

An expression Heather couldn't interpret flashed across Colton's face. He started to say something, then stopped. "You got me," he said.

CHAPTER SEVEN

They veered down the winding dirt road, two weeks later, on their way into town—Ty, Katie and Heather, shoulder to shoulder, in Ty's silver, four-wheel-drive Dodge pickup. To their left, crisscrossed posts, supporting long pine poles, formed jack fences which stood along the lone road, the sole signs of civilization in this rolling wilderness of sagebrush and prairie grass.

"What a week," Ty said. Minus a hat today, he'd combed his normally unruly locks into a plastered-back style. The stuff he'd used to encourage his thick mane to lay flat made it look practically black.

Heather liked his hair better when it just curled naturally as it usually did. Combed or uncombed, though, Ty had beautiful hair. "I'll say—pretty wild week. Mom will never believe I helped prepare three huge meals a day." How could these people eat all that food and not gain a ton of weight? She guessed they just ran it off. Her own jeans hung looser, trying to keep up with her friends.

"Kevin will be surprised you learned to drive a tractor," Katie said.

"That will be a surprise," Heather returned.

They rounded a curve and she clutched the armrest to keep from squashing Katie. Here the old fence left them, pivoting toward the mountains which were dark with timber.

"You'll have to carry your antelope blinders," Ty said.

"Slug him for me, will you?" Heather told Katie.

"Okay. If you insist." She punched him in the arm.

He kiddingly rubbed where she'd hit him. "Oh! Ouch! Injured for life."

As busy as the Taggerts were they always had time to pull a prank or enjoy a good laugh. Ty, Katie and Wells had kidded Heather continually about getting the tractor and mowing machine stuck in the ditch while she watched an antelope graze in the next field.

She sighed. Colton hadn't been around much to kid, talk— nothing. He'd spent most of his time at the home ranch. The couple of times she'd seen him, he'd been distant and reserved and she wondered how things would've been had she reacted differently that day in Charlie's cabin. At least worrying about Colton kept her from brooding about Charlie. She'd thought it best not to tell Katie about the "missing calf." Colton hadn't seemed too concerned, so why should she be?

Ty's smile brought Heather back to the present. She hadn't realized she'd been staring at him all the time she'd been thinking about Colton. She returned the smile, then looked away.

"Ooh. So sober. What ya thinking about?" he asked.

Quick. What would he believe? "Image."

"No wonder you looked depressed. Nah, just kidding. He's coming along good, don't you think?"

Under Ty's direction, Heather had ridden the horse a lot during the past week. With her fall fresh in mind, she'd been frightened at first. Only her determination to prove herself to

Kevin and Ty's constant hounding had kept her from giving up. How she'd longed to ride a dependable ranch horse while she and Ty checked fences or doctored sick calves, but he wouldn't let her.

"Image better do well or I'll never hear the end of it. Katie, you didn't tell me Ty could be so bossy." Heather rolled her eyes.

"Really. I thought I had."

They laughed.

With all Ty's lecturing, it amazed Heather that they remained such good friends. He'd been upset the other day when she'd left Image and slipped off with Colton, but it hadn't lasted long. Once she began working her horse again, all seemed forgiven. It was as if he wanted her to succeed as much as she did.

Ty swerved to miss a gopher and Katie leaned into Heather.

"Slow down," Katie grumbled. "You're making me sick."

Peering down his nose at his sister, Ty said, "You didn't need to come, you know."

"Yes, I did," she countered.

Just how Katie had contrived her presence remained a mystery. Blackmail may have played a part. Actually, neither brother nor sister was above such things. Had it not been for Ty, Heather might have been with Colton right now.

"No, you didn't," Ty said.

"Mom said I could."

"Only after you laid a guilt trip on her. 'Everyone else is going,'" he said in a high voice. "Why didn't you hitch a ride with Colton?"

"Colton? Are you crazy?"

Heather wouldn't have minded. At lunch earlier, during one of his rare appearances, he'd said, "Anyone know where I can get a date tonight for dinner and a movie?"

"Heather's with me," Ty had said, squaring his shoulders. "She wants to help me pick out a new hat. Then we're going to dinner and a show."

Even though Ty had interfered with her chance to set things straight with Colton, Heather couldn't be angry, not after all he'd done to help with Image.

As Heather and the others drew closer to town, small ranches sprouted up, like patches of green on a lumpy tweed carpet. Heather studied one now with its cluster of log buildings—someone's home in the middle of nowhere.

A reddish blur in the side mirror redirected Heather's attention and she watched as it grew larger—Colton's hondurous maroon 1962 Corvette. Last week he'd hurriedly shown her the car that had cost him three summers working construction. It suited him perfectly.

"Show-off," snorted Katie as Colton honked the horn. He nodded a greeting before trying to pass. Heather's heart fluttered.

Instead of letting Colton go around, Ty sped up.

Heather gasped.

Glancing at her, he slowed and let his brother by.

"I'll bet he's headed to see Jennifer Stoddard," Katie announced. "They've been going steady for three years now, or so she thinks. She'd just die if she knew about all of Colton's other girlfriends." Katie covered a chuckle with her hand. "I'd love to tell her."

Ty glanced at Heather, then turned his eyes back to the road. A muscle in his cheek twitched.

"How far is it to town?" she asked.

"About ten more miles," he said.

For nine of the ten Heather thought about Colton. Surely Katie had exaggerated about all of Colton's girlfriends. Actually, she'd rather he had several and not just one special girl.

Closer to town, the landscape changed. Instead of sage-covered range, lush green hay fields now covered the foreground. Big, expensive-looking machines dropped hay in great swaths. Bright metal gates hung on lopsided pole fences, and sparkling water brimmed nearby ditches.

Beaver Springs Mercantile stood smack-dab in the middle of town. Since no sidewalk paved the way, Ty pulled right up in front of the log store. Heather glanced down the street. Parking posed little problem in Beaver Springs.

She climbed out of the truck and followed Ty and Katie into the mercantile. It was bordered on one side by a bar and on the other by an abandoned corral. As she passed through the doorway, she peered up at a sign which read "Elevation 5,690; Population 1,658" and wondered if they repainted the sign every time a new baby was born.

The store contained a fine selection of hats, ropes and chewing tobacco—just about all the necessities. The dark wood floor squeaked when they walked on it and an aroma of leather and pine filled the room.

Ty fancied a buckskin-colored straw hat with a tall brim and fuzzy orange feather sticking out from a braided band. After obtaining approval from the girls, he reached into his back pocket for his wallet.

While he visited with the smiling salesman, Heather stepped to the counter. "This is my treat, remember," she told Ty and started to pass the man some cash.

"Not on your life." Ty took the money from her hand and slipped it into her purse. "Jed, her money's no good. Take it out of this." He produced a fifty-dollar bill.

"I told you he wouldn't let you pay," Katie whispered to Heather as the trio left the store.

"Oh, there's that cool bookstore I told you about," Katie said, dragging Heather across the street.

"Okay," Ty said. "You two go in there. I'll meet you back here in half an hour."

The bookstore was just what Katie had promised. It had a smattering of everything a large city store would have, but seemed more homey and personal with its little sitting area and close arrangement of books that invited patrons to touch. The owner made Heather feel like a special family friend. She and Katie purchased seven books between them.

"Ready?" Ty said as he walked into the store. "Hi, Debbie."

"Hi, Ty. Nice hat."

"Do you like it?" Tipping it off his head, he showed his new purchase to her.

"Your hair!" Heather gasped. "What did you do to your hair?"

All of Ty's black curls had vanished. His beautiful hair was a dark mat against his head.

Both Katie and Debbie stared at Heather.

"I like it," the store owner said.

"It was a haircut or a dog license." Katie rubbed the top of Ty's head.

"I like it too," Heather said. "It's just . . . different." Why should the length of Ty's hair matter to her? It didn't really.

Ty eased on his hat. "Fits better without all that hair." He stood back so Heather and Katie could go out. "Ladies." He offered each an arm. "I was starting to look like a girl."

Heather took hold of his biceps. "With those muscles, no one would ever make that mistake."

Beneath the hat, Ty's face colored.

Debbie chuckled and waved to the trio as they left the store, heading for Ty's pickup.

"No. You first," Katie told Heather, positioning her friend next to her brother.

A tour of the town followed. Katie pointed out the high spots.

"There's the *Daily Courier*. Best little newspaper in the West, where in addition to the state and national gossip, one can learn who's visiting who in the community, and . . ."

"What we're having for school lunch on any given day," Ty added.

Heather noted that many of the buildings in Beaver Springs were free standing, not sharing common walls with the neighboring businesses like where she came from. Some of them looked like they'd been around since Billy the Kid's time.

"There's Flossie's Second Hand Store and there's our church," Katie said. "On warm days we hold class outside."

"Almost makes it bearable," Ty said, receiving a glare from Katie and a giggle from Heather.

"Out there's the cemetery and that's the post office." Katie pointed. "Oh, and Wells Fargo Bank. It got robbed once. The guy walked off with a lot of Taggert money. No one could ever figure out how he knew Dad had just deposited all that cash from the big cattle sale."

Ty slowed the truck to allow a girl about his age to cross the street in front of them. The blonde turned and waved, as did Ty, and Heather felt a prickle in her stomach. She rubbed it. Shouldn't have skipped breakfast.

"Now right there," Ty said, "that's where we'll be going to the movie tonight. If something flies over your head, duck. It's probably a bat. Rumor has it we're getting a new theater soon, but we've heard that for years."

"There's our school," Katie said. "We go there from first grade right on through high school." Heather noted a building about the size of the gymnasium at her own school.

"It's pretty small," Ty added. "But there are advantages. If you can bounce a basketball, they put you on the team."

"Did you play?" Heather asked.

"He can't bounce a ball," Katie said.

"How would you like to walk home?" he returned.

Katie put on a repentant expression.

Ty turned to Heather and explained. "What with training horses and stuff, I couldn't take the time."

"Colton did though," Katie said. "Our team did really good. They beat all the bigger schools in our division and took the conference."

While Heather tried to imagine how Colton would look in a basketball uniform, Ty said, "I want to show you something, Heather."

They passed Joe's Fix-it Shop where buckrakes of varied descriptions congregated. Heather had learned buckrakes were reversed tractors with large oak forks on the front. Apparently the ranchers were getting their equipment in shape before haying started in earnest.

Ty's truck rounded the corner and Heather marveled at the beauty of the purplish mountains in the distance.

"What do you think of her?" Ty said as he brought the truck to a halt. "Isn't she something?"

Heather looked where Ty pointed. The mare stood in a pasture with several other horses, but he didn't need to single her out. Heather knew which one she had to be. She was taller than a Quarter Horse had any right to be—and lanky. Her sloping shoulder, straight back and muscled hindquarters were all in perfect thirds, and her long arched neck displayed a delicate, almost dished head. To top it off, she was the beautiful golden-red, sorrel color. No wonder Ty was desperate to possess her. The mare's name, Lady Roxanna, was ideal for her. Ty called her Roxie.

"She's magnificent," Heather whispered almost reverently. "Do you think you'll be able to buy her?"

"Dad wants Ty to save his money for college this fall," Katie said.

"I can go to college anytime. A horse like this comes along only if someone up there . . ."—he glanced skyward—". . . smiles on you."

The mare wandered to the fence. Ty slipped out of the truck. Heather joined him for a better look.

"Can't you see the potential?" he said. "She could be the foundation mare for a whole new string of blooded horses on the ranch—an excellent investment."

"She's beautiful. She really is," Heather said, "but your education is important too. Didn't you say you want to be a vet? Maybe you can do both."

"Maybe," Ty said, as he stroked the mare's neck, "but not likely."

With a backward look of longing, Ty maneuvered Heather to his side of the truck and opened the door for her. She slid across the seat ahead of Ty to sit between brother and sister again.

The tour of the town ended in front of what appeared to be an ancient schoolhouse, complete with bell. Heather half expected to see the schoolmaster step out and usher them back in from recess. Instead, a heavyset woman with a toothless grin and bandanna-wrapped head waved from the open front door.

"That's Ruth," Ty said as he returned the greeting. "She puts on a terrific feed. Truckers drive for miles out of their way to sink their teeth into one of her specially cooked steaks."

"You'll like this place," Katie added. "It's got tons of great junk in it, and it's super old."

Heather followed behind Ty and Katie. As they entered, Ruth put her arm around the boy, giving him a squeeze. "It's about time you came to see me, Ty—you too, Katie. What'll you have? We've got ham and turkey tonight. Who's the pretty little thing with you? Is she your girlfriend, Ty? Have you been holding out on old Ruth? Hey, that's a swell looking hat."

It was plain to see the uselessness of trying to talk when Ruth had something to say. Ty just stood there grinning.

While Ruth rattled on about local happenings, Heather surveyed the room. Faded, leather-bound books crowded makeshift shelves, and there was a old-time typewriter, phonograph and a funny looking vacuum cleaner with a huge cloth bag at the back. Yellowed cards with the ABC's carefully scribed upon them hung above a blackboard. Charlie Russell calendar prints adorned the wooden walls. Desks, stuck together on runners, bordered the room, and an old upright piano stood abandoned in one corner.

Ruth seated Ty, Heather and Katie at a large table beside an elderly couple, with whom Ty immediately struck up a conversation. Several others came in and sat at tables close by.

"Ty," someone yelled, "how's that bay mare coming along?"

While Ruth and the two girls Heather guessed were her daughters readied the meal, the older woman called greetings to everyone who arrived, carrying on several conversations at once.

Heather couldn't help but stare. A plate was placed before her, as were a glass and silverware. Nothing matched. The food was served in large dishes from which everyone helped themselves like at a huge family gathering.

At first Heather didn't notice Colton. She was too busy assessing the gorgeous creature strutting beside him.

"That's Jennifer Stoddard," Katie reported, nudging Heather. "She's the one I told you about."

Heather felt Ty's eyes upon her. Her face went hot.

"Pretty," she said.

Ty looked away.

Was the meeting planned or purely accidental? Heather could only guess. Colton strolled up and introduced Jennifer to Heather.

Wow! Heather doubted she'd ever seen a girl so striking—not even her friend from back home, the boy magnet, Sheila. Tall, about 5'9", Jennifer was model thin, with long, shapely legs and a tiny waist. Her short, auburn hair fell low on her forehead and feathered back from her delicate face. Her heavily lashed brown eyes complemented a slightly upturned nose and full lips. She wore tight white jeans and a pink shirt, bare at the midriff when she raised her arms. Already Heather felt like an ugly stepsister beside Cinderella and the prince, but she managed a friendly hello.

Peering down over the tip of her shoulder at Heather, Jennifer merely nodded. "Come on, Colton. Tiffany and Sam are waiting over there." She took Colton by the arm. He showed little resistance, which left Heather stinging.

Katie flashed an exaggerated smile. "Isn't she precious?"

Throughout the remainder of the meal, Heather tried to make small talk, even act cheerful, but her food wouldn't go down and her eyes continually sought the other table.

"Do you know that guy over there, Heather? He kinda reminds me of someone I knew at school, but it's you he can't take his eyes off of."

"Where?" Ty said.

Heather snuck a quick look. Tall, thin—too thin. Pale—real pale. "No. I don't know him. He's not watching me, is he, Katie?"

"Well, every time I look over there, he's staring over here. It's a sure bet he's not watching me and I hope he's not watching Ty. It has to be you."

Periodically, Heather peeked over at the stranger. He appeared to be a little older than herself and might have been handsome except for a sort of haunted, lonely look on his face and a lack of muscle on his bones. During one stolen glance, Heather got the impression his interest lay in Ty, Katie and even Colton.

At least wondering about the stranger gave her something to take her mind off Colton and the fabulous Jennifer.

When the meal finally concluded, Heather wanted to cheer. As she, Ty and Katie left, Heather felt as if someone watched her every step. She wished she'd worn her new blue slacks instead of these beige ones. The blue ones fit just right and the dark color made her look thinner.

The movie, a Tarzan remake, proved tolerable and the theater only half as dismal as Ty had described. Heather didn't see one bat, but she did see a couple of two-legged rats snuggled closely together three rows ahead.

CHAPTER EIGHT

Heather sat up wide-eyed in the old brass bed. Darkness hung around her like soggy air in a sauna. At least she hadn't screamed this time. She recalled with a shudder the horrible face in her dreams again—the one that had caused her to make such a scene the night she'd first arrived—the one she imagined to be Charlie's. Glancing at the illuminated dial on the travel clock next to her bed, she noted the time read 2:10. Everyone else in the house must be asleep. She hadn't heard Colton come in. Maybe he'd returned to the home ranch, or perhaps she'd dreamed through his arrival.

Fluffing her pillow, she lay back. Her mind stuck in high gear and replayed her current worries. No matter how hard she tried, she simply couldn't explain the missing painting or what had sounded like dragging chains at Charlie's. Apparently repressing her thoughts during the day only forced them to surface at night. Perhaps she'd be haunted by these same nightmares until she found some explanation for the strange happenings.

She rearranged the covers and turned onto her side—stared at the backs of her eyelids. Still sleep eluded her. Image. Another worry. The horse would never be ready for the fair in the fall. She'd disappoint Kevin. Groaning, she pulled the pillow over her face. She had to get some sleep. Maybe . . . maybe warm milk would help—never had in the past, but she'd try anything.

Reaching for her robe, she decided against it. She'd only be a minute and with these flannel pajamas, she'd feel too bulky wearing both. At last she'd found a use for the red pj's with the feet on them. Kevin had given them to her as a gag, but she'd tossed them into her suitcase at the last minute. They'd proved cozy during the cool Montana nights.

On her way to the refrigerator, she stopped short. What was that? Listening intently, she stood fixed, ready to run. A minute passed before she identified the sound. She shook her head, angry at her fear, and tiptoed into the hall. She flipped on the light and knelt beside a cardboard box. Smoky, busy arranging the nursery, nuzzled four wailing newborn kittens—two spotted, one gray, and one coal black. Heather picked up the gray kitten, holding it to her face. She felt its tiny claws and the warmth of its body.

Suddenly the outside door opened. Knowing the unlikelihood of a dignified retreat in her bright red pajamas, Heather stayed where she sat and smiled pathetically into Colton's lopsided grin.

"I couldn't sleep," she muttered and nestled the kitten in the box next to its mother.

"I didn't know storks came adorned in red pajamas. I take it those are pajamas." Colton raised his brows.

Her face burned, probably matching her apparel. She stood and searched for her jacket on the cluttered coat rack beside her.

When she turned back, he still grinned. She couldn't help but notice a couple of auburn hairs on the shoulder of his black leather flight jacket. "You're shedding," she said.

His mouth twisted. He reached up to brush the hair off. "She was my second choice."

Heather looked away. She wished she could believe him, but if Colton had really wanted to be with her instead of Jennifer, he should've shown more pain and suffering. Of course, from what Heather had observed, Jennifer probably wouldn't understand the word "no."

"I think I can sleep now." She turned to leave.

Colton caught her arm. He stepped closer.

Tingles crept up the back of her neck.

"You don't believe me, do you?" he said.

She glanced at his hand on her arm, then at his handsome face. Her heart accelerated into flirting mode, but she managed to say, "You had a pretty good time."

He let her arm slip through his fingers as she backed away. "You noticed."

"I'm bashful, not blind."

"Jen and I've been going together for a long time." His voice carried a tone of regret.

Drawing her coat securely around her neck, Heather said, "I take it Jennifer wouldn't have liked me going in her place."

Colton removed his jacket and slung it over his shoulder. "Probably not. I'd have been in the doghouse, but it would've been worth it."

"Somehow I can't picture you with a name like Spot or Rover."

Colton laughed. Leaning against the doorjamb in his blue cotton shirt and tight jeans, he looked like a model. "Ruff. Ruff."

She rolled her eyes. "You don't seem to care if . . ." What Colton did and who he did it with was none of her business.

"What?" he asked.

"Nothing."

"Come on. Tell me." He straightened.

"No."

Hanging his jacket on the coat rack, he walked toward her. She backed up into a large chest freezer and jumped forward, startled.

"Tell me." Colton grabbed her and tried to tickle out a confession.

"Stop. Stop it," Heather giggled, struggling half-heartedly to get away. Then, unable to think of anything else to say to relieve her predicament, she let the truth tumble out.

"I was just wondering how you would've behaved if it had been me with you last night? There, I said it."

One dark brow raised seductively, and he let her go. "Wanna see?"

She dodged Colton's playful grasp. "I'll take a rain check. You've had enough attention for one night. See you tomorrow, okay?"

Before he could answer, she slipped away, beating a hasty retreat to the safety of her bedroom. Why did she keep running away? Well, could it have been Jennifer, or the fact that Colton flirted with every female between the ages of six and sixty, or could it be she still had feelings for David? She did get some pleasure imagining what might have happened if she'd stayed.

She drifted into restless sleep. What seemed like minutes later, she heard knocking at her door and Ty's voice. "Heather, wake up. Grab Image and come with me."

CHAPTER
NINE

W hat time is it?" Heather asked, stumbling to the door to
open it.

"A little before five. Come on. Daylight's burning." He smiled.
"Great pajamas."

She glanced down at herself, shook her head and sighed.
"Never mind."

That was the first morning of many in which Ty appeared at a
time when normal people would have been enjoying their best
sleep. Heather could never remember being so tired.

While Katie and the rest of the family kept up with their
normal responsibilities—mostly haying these days—Ty and
Heather somehow ended up with unusual jobs. She suspected
he'd planned it that way in order to subject Image to new
challenges.

* * *

"I think it's watered," she said, studying a huge field of
standing water.

"Looks good, doesn't it? We weren't able to irrigate like this
before we got hold of Charlie's spring. We'll raise hay here now."

Drover, Ty's buckskin gelding, splashed across the field.
"Coming?" Ty called.

"Where?"

"To change the headgate—turn the water onto that piece of ground over there." He pointed.

"Image doesn't like water."

Ty cocked his head. "So . . . Look at this as an opportunity."

"To get tossed?"

"No. To get him used to water."

"I'll get dumped."

"No you won't. You're a good rider. Use your legs." Ty circled back behind Image. "Kick him." He brought his lariat down on the gelding's rump.

Image leaped in the air, landing on all fours in the standing water.

"Ty, darn you," Heather squealed. "I bent a nail." She sent him a dirty look.

Mud dripped from the brim of Ty's new hat and covered his face and shirt.

As she swayed back and forth in fits of laughter, Heather gripped the front of her saddle for support. "Serves you right."

"Got him into the water, didn't it?"

Heather nodded, fighting back another giggle.

Easing off his hat, Ty shook most of the muddy water from it. He wiped his face with the cleanest part of his sleeve. "Let's get that headgate moved."

"Aye, aye, sir." Heather saluted and clucked to Image.

Mud came to Image's knees—higher on Drover's—but the black gelding sloshed ahead without further incident. Heather grinned to herself. Progress.

Moving cattle from one mountain pasture to another took the next pretty ordinary Tuesday and Wednesday, which were easy compared to Thursday.

"Ty," Wells said, over a midnight snack of apples and cheese. "Gus called this evening."

Heather and Ty had just come from the barn after a day herding cattle. "Gus?" he asked.

"That rodeo stock supplier who pastures his animals next to the home ranch." Wells placed another stack of sliced cheese on a plate in the middle of the kitchen table.

"Oh, you mean big Gus." Ty held his arms out to the side and flexed his muscles.

"Yeah. Big Gus. Anyway, a couple of our colts got rounded up with his stock. They'd used them as bareback broncs for a whole month before they noticed their brands."

Ty stopped chewing. "I'll bet one of the colts is Sunset's and the other is probably out of that bally-faced mare you bought off Frank Lodge. I figured Dallas had hauled them off to the auction. They were nice colts, especially Sunset's."

"Could be. I don't keep close track of the colts like you do, but will you take the Chevy over there in the morning and pick them up? We could use extra horses this summer, after you gentle them, of course."

"Sure, Dad." He sat up straight in his chair, a grin teasing his lips.

"Better take Drover. Our colts are running with Gus's extra stock. You'll have to cut 'em out."

"Dad?" Ty glanced at Heather.

Uh oh. She squinched down in her chair.

"I'll take Heather with me, okay?"

So much for sleeping in. These Montanans never slept. Must be some law against it. She covered a yawn with her hand.

"Good idea. Let her ride that gray mare," Wells said.

"She's been riding her own horse." Ty walked to the refrigerator, returning to the table with a carton of milk. He retrieved three plastic glasses.

"Really?" Wells poured milk for the three of them.

"Yeah. He's not too bad."

"Sometimes," Heather rolled her eyes.

Wells chuckled. "Okay," he said and held up his glass.

Ty clinked his against Wells's, then held it for Heather to click hers. "It's a go then."

* * *

Sure enough, at five a.m. sharp, Ty tapped on Heather's door.

She leaped out of bed. "I'm up. I'm up," she yelled, rubbing her eyes.

Image worked himself into a good sweat that day, as did Heather. Not only were the young horses wild as teenagers on a Saturday night, but the stock from which Image and Drover tried to separate the colts seemed to take delight in leading the youngsters off in a wild game of tag.

"Image won't like riding in the truck with them," Heather protested after they'd driven the snorting, kicking colts up the loading chute into the two-ton truck.

Ty's eyes narrowed.

"I know. I know." For Ty's benefit, Heather stuck out her lower lip in a fake pout. "This is an opportunity."

"Tell you what. I'll put Drover in next so he can keep the peace."

Apparently Drover did. No temper tantrums erupted on the drive home, and Image walked quietly into the barn, head down, when they arrived, way after dark.

Next morning's agenda consisted of rounding up sheep—ten head—wild. But at least Ty let her sleep until 5:30.

Once more they loaded Image and Drover into the back of the Chevy truck. Heather knew better than to say anything about Image not wanting to load.

They drove up a valley Ty called The Muddy as far as the road lasted. Pine-covered mountains rose on either side. A hawk soared above while gophers scampered across the rutted, rock-covered road.

"How did you find out about these sheep?" she asked.

"Colton and Dallas saw them while they were practice flying."

"I didn't think you raised sheep."

"Used to. We had about two thousand, but decided to get out of the lambing operation several years ago. We must have missed those few when we rounded up the others."

They unloaded Drover and Image, and after about an hour's horseback ride, Ty said, "There they are."

Heather squinted. Had it not been for their white color—well, actually sort of a weathered beige—she may not have spotted them, but then the entire ledge seemed to move as the sheep bunched and headed up the mountainside.

Heather thought of the phrase "sure-footed as a mountain goat." Oh dear. Image could be difficult to ride on level ground.

"They're huge."

"It's the wool. They haven't been sheared for probably two years."

Image must have thought they looked large too. He took one step forward then backed up, setting his feet as if bolted to the ground.

She grimaced. "I don't suppose they're gonna scurry on down here and jump into the truck, are they?"

"Not likely." He stared up the mountain. "No place to maneuver and it's pretty steep up there. Drover and I will see if we can drive them down."

"Image and I will wait here," Heather replied.

The sheep watched for a moment as Ty and his horse headed up a ravine, then they scampered off, staying just out of reach.

"This could take a while," Ty yelled back.

Several times Ty and Drover climbed farther up the hill to come down above the sheep. The woolly animals started down, but then one or another of them would break from the herd and lead the others back up the hill.

After riding his horse until sweat dripped off its buckskin neck, Ty still hadn't succeeded in gathering the sheep, even though they were panting beneath their heavy wool coats.

"Let me switch you horses. Drover's about had it."

"Really? Hear that, Image? Ty wants to ride you." She rubbed the gelding's neck. "What's that?" She cupped her hand around her ear and leaned forward in her saddle, a western one today. "Oh, he says he doesn't like new riders."

Ty shook his head. "None of your sass." He climbed off Drover.

"I don't know, Ty. Do you trust Image on that cliff?"

"You bet. He and I are buds, aren't we, fella?"

Image laid his ears back at the boy's approach.

"Say! Is that any way to act?" Ty rubbed the gelding's neck, then swung into the saddle and legged the black horse forward.

After one preliminary buck, Image dutifully lowered his head and trudged up the mountain.

Heather remained by the exhausted buckskin. "Why wouldn't my horse do that for me?"

The black gelding gave a decent imitation of a cow pony and was finally able to help Ty gather the tired sheep and drive them down the mountain. Image even got to release a little frustration by nipping at their stubby tails as he urged them along.

Ty and Heather loaded the sheep into the truck, then Drover, and finally Image. The black gelding stood quietly, his ears alternately flattened against his neck or pivoted forward as if trying to decide whether the big beasts were friends or enemies.

Later, in the barn, he dozed while Heather brushed his sweat-stained body, something he'd rarely tolerated in the past.

"Lookin' good," she told her horse. "You haven't lost weight with all this riding—even getting a nice little layer of muscle right here." She scratched his back. "Kevin will be immmmpressed." She yawned. "No pampering on this ranch. If we manage to survive, I guess we'll be better off for having had the experience—at least that's what Mom would say—even if we're so sleepy we can't wiggle."

A person's mind can play tricks on them when they get that tired. Perhaps exhaustion did play a part in what Heather thought she saw several nights later—three weeks after her arrival.

CHAPTER
TEN

The mystery novel slipped from her fingers as Heather sprang from the green tweed sofa in the Taggert living room. She peeked out the window and let the breath she'd been holding escape. The wind bent the branches of a nearby pine against the ranch house eaves. That's what had caused the eerie tapping.

Normally buzzing with activity, the house was lonely tonight. Wells and Ty had gone to bed. Colton had returned to the home ranch, and an orthodontist appointment and shopping for school clothes had provided an excuse for Bea and Katie to stay in a motel in the city.

She returned to the couch, curling her legs up beside her. As tired as she was, Heather should have been able to sleep, but remembering the vision of Charlie that sometimes haunted her dreams, she put off going to bed.

Perhaps she should have taken Bea and Katie up on their offer to go along on the three hundred-mile round trip to one of the few orthodontists in the area, but Heather had thought then and guessed she still did that she could shop in a city anytime. Besides, Bea and Katie deserved time together without having a tag-along.

Heather flipped a page of the Mary Higgins Clark mystery lying in her lap and wondered about her choice of lonely, late-night reading. Perhaps she should read the letter from her folks again. She slipped the envelope from between the pages of the book and pulled out the letter.

A roll of thunder and rain pelting the windows reminded her of a more serious concern. Even though Ty had insisted that time in the pasture would do Image good, she should have never left the horse unsheltered. Of course, neither she nor Ty had foreseen this bad of weather in late June.

Now lightning illuminated Heather's surroundings. How could Ty and Wells sleep through such a storm? As much as she hated the idea, she had to do it.

Outside, wind and rain whipped at the scarf around her neck. She poked the plaid material into her coat, then pulled a stocking cap more securely over her ears. The storm almost swallowed the cone of light she carried in her gloved hand.

Ty's company would have been welcome, but Heather wasn't about to wake him. He'd only go on about spoiling her horse. And anyway, she didn't want to make a big deal out of the whole thing.

Heather grabbed a halter and lead rope from the barn and ducked out into the rain.

Partner stood with his back to the storm, head low, almost asleep. Not so with Image. Heather's flashlight shone on flared nostrils and wide, white-rimmed eyes.

Hoping she could catch him, Heather walked forward. She tried to keep her voice calm and steady. Image snorted and lunged. Heather jumped aside to keep the big horse from knocking her to the ground.

The skin at the back of her neck tightened. "Go ahead and get pneumonia then," she screamed. "See if I care."

The words were barely out of her mouth when Heather groaned. She shouldn't even think things like that. She didn't want anything to happen to Image. Kevin would not only lose the money he'd paid, but she'd never be able to prove her worth to her stepfather. Besides, she'd never want Image hurt.

Heading for the horse again, Heather promised herself that if she couldn't catch him this time, she'd go for help.

Finally she cornered Image between the fence and a branding chute. She stretched out her hand and for a moment he hesitated. Just as she was about to drape the rope around his long, arched neck, a bolt of lightning shattered the sky. The gelding whirled, cantered a few steps and instead of running at Heather as he had before, headed straight for the huge pole fence.

A clap of thunder muffled Heather's scream. "No, Image. No!" Total helplessness anchored her to the ground.

The horse gathered his sleek muscles, rose high and leaped up and over the five-foot fence. Her mouth hanging open, Heather watched as Image vanished into the darkness.

What should she do? If she ran for help, she'd lose track of the horse entirely. She had no choice. She'd have to go after Image.

Luckily, Partner showed no objection to being caught. Heather pulled off her gloves to buckle Image's halter on the Palomino's head. She led him out through the gate.

No time to saddle up, but a quick trip to the barn produced another rope and halter. The flashlight slipped from Heather's pocket as she leaped onto Partner's back and raced after Image. She probably wouldn't find the horse, but she didn't know what else to do.

Partner seemed to sense where his friend was going. Heather gave him his head. She lowered herself against the horse's neck to shield her face from the biting rain, staying put until her back ached from the strain of the miles. Luckily she had lots of bareback riding experience. Until a few years ago she didn't even own a saddle.

She straightened and searched first one pocket, then the other, for her gloves. When she couldn't find them, she wiggled the sleeves of her coat down as far on her hands as possible.

Straining her eyes in the darkness, she thought she saw something move in front of her, but couldn't be certain.

When had she left the house? Had it been around 1:30? What time was it now?

Partner stopped abruptly and Heather grabbed his mane, crying out as a sharp object caught her cheek. She dropped lower against Partner's neck and felt something, probably tree branches, yank the red stocking cap from her head. She reached for it. Too late.

Heather's wet hair plastered the sides of her head as Partner trotted forward. Climbing, he slowed on the rougher terrain.

More accustomed to the darkness now, Heather distinguished trees and cliffs on the skyline. A noise ahead, sounding like a horse's shoe hitting a rock, trained her eyes in that direction. Had he been a color other than black, she would've probably seen him sooner. Image. She hoped he felt as exhausted as she did, so maybe she could catch him.

Shivering, Heather remembered that most of a person's body heat is lost through the top of the head. With a shaking, cold hand she loosened the scarf from her neck and tied it around her head. The extra halter slipped down her arm and she noted with a frown that she'd lost the lead rope. At least she still had the halter.

Heather heard branches cracking ahead. Damp leaves brushed her face and shoulders. When Partner broke into a trot in a clearing, cold air hit her. She felt for her scarf. Darn. Now it was missing.

All at once Heather forgot the rain drizzling down her back and Kevin's show horse running free. She sat corpse still upon Partner's back, staring into the distance. There in the darkness of the storm a light shone brightly, just like Katie had said. Now Heather knew where Image had gone. He'd been here before.

Lightning cast a deathly glow on the face of Charlie's cabin, highlighting the ghastly radiance that shone from the window.

As if hypnotized, Heather urged Partner closer. No illusion— a light flickered. Katie had not imagined it. She wasn't imagining it either.

Suddenly Heather sensed movement. She half expected to see Image. But something other than Kevin's renegade horse caused her throat to tighten. Another flash of lightning revealed the unearthly presence of a grisly personage standing at Partner's head. She screamed. Her horse whirled from the object.

Struggling to keep her seat on the Palomino's slippery wet back, she had only an instant to note the pasty white features of the intruder and the dark holes where eyes should have been.

Her fingers slipped through Partner's mane and she struck the ground. Whether she fainted or was knocked out, she would never know.

* * *

Dawn had come when Heather regained consciousness. She lay still, moving only her eyes as she peered cautiously from side to side. She sat up straight. How long had she been out?

Gratefully, she was still in one piece and the rain had stopped. Except for Partner who remained nearby, searching for grass, she was alone. Whatever she'd seen earlier had vanished without a trace.

Pulling herself to a sitting position, she tried to decipher what had happened. When she stood, a sharp pain in her forehead reminded her of her fall.

She walked to Partner and rubbed his short, thick neck. "What a good boy. You didn't run off and leave me like another horse, who shall go unmentioned, would have." Her ears pricked for any alien sound.

Image was probably long gone and she didn't know where she'd ever find him. How could she face Kevin?

Her eyes sought Charlie's place. In the day it looked far less chilling, but still she shuddered. Whatever she'd seen last night and this house had to be connected. After all, there'd been that light in the window. Although curious, no way would she check it out by herself—not now.

A branch broke behind her. She grabbed Partner's halter, but couldn't summon the strength to swing on. Her heart threatening to leap from her chest, Heather turned to face whatever was coming.

CHAPTER
ELEVEN

Ty's easy grin met Heather's wide-eyed stare. "I guess you're gonna tell me you couldn't sleep." He dismounted a big bay horse she remembered he'd called Joker.

Relief weakened her knees, but excitement that reinforcements had arrived sent her running. She clung to him in a huge hug. Strong arms wrapped tentatively around her. Although she'd been glad to see him, her reaction surprised even her.

"If I'd known I'd get such a reception," Ty stammered, "I'd have left earlier."

Heather swallowed hard. "You must have left pretty early as it was. How did you find me?"

He cleared his throat. "There ain't many of us old trackers left in these parts," he drawled, then switched to his normal voice, "but between sloppy footsteps, broken branches and these . . ." She followed his nod to where her scarf and Image's lead rope wound around the horn of Ty's saddle. ". . . you left a trail any greenhorn could've followed." He pulled her gloves, hat and the flashlight from his saddlebags. "Yours?"

"Just the gloves and hat. The light belongs to you. It must have dropped out of my pocket. Lucky it didn't break."

"Actually, it came in handy. Do you want these gloves and hat right now, or would you like Joker to carry them?" He lifted the top of a saddle bag.

"I'd probably just drop them again. Yeah, stick them in there. Thanks, Ty, and thanks for coming." She studied her thumb, then bit at a hangnail. "Actually, I should be mad. This is all your fault, you know."

Ty hooked the stirrup over the horn, then pulled up on the strap to tighten the bay's girth. "My fault?"

"You and your 'Let's let Image stay out for a while.'" Heather rubbed Joker's nose.

"Did I say that?"

"You did."

Flopping the stirrup down, Ty glanced at Heather. "I'm sorry. I really am. If it makes you feel any better, I did my share of worrying about you."

He reached over and touched her cheek where the deep scratch from last night's ride cut across her face. His hand lingered, then moved to the back of her neck, beneath the mass of matted hair. "When the storm woke me and I found you and Image gone . . . How'd he get out anyway?"

"He jumped," she said, telling herself this was her good buddy Ty, not his dashing older brother.

"That huge fence! Are you kidding me?" The hand on her neck moved, but only slightly. The button on the cuff of his Levi jacket entangled itself in the locks of her hair.

No doubt about which brother stood next to her now. Colton was always so smooth.

She held onto her hair at the scalp while Ty shed his jacket and used both hands to release her.

"I wish I were kidding." She tried to pick up a thread of the prior conversation to keep from blushing. "Then Image wouldn't be running off somewhere by himself."

"He'll show up. Where would he go?" Ty secured his jacket to the rear of the saddle.

Heather surveyed the wide expanse of land surrounding her. A few cows dotted the horizon. She supposed they were Taggert cattle and for an instant wondered about the pure white cow and her calf. "Where would he go? Are you serious?"

"Well, horses don't like traipsing off by themselves. They show up sooner or later." He fingered the rope hanging from the front of his horse's saddle. "Where did you see him last?"

"Here, right before . . . before . . . ." Chewing her lip, Heather walked to Partner, who still grazed nearby. "Ty, I saw something really strange last night." She pulled the collar of her parka around her neck. Suddenly she felt cold.

"Like what?" Stooping, Ty picked up the extra halter Heather had dropped when she'd fallen and placed it over the saddlehorn. Then he led the bay over to Partner.

Heather flashed an uneasy grin. "It was . . . well, kinda like a person, but not exactly."

He stared at her so funny that she didn't mention the light in the window of Charlie's house. "You're talkin' like Katie."

"It sounds weird, but I know what I saw." She slipped out of her coat and tied its sleeves around her waist.

"Lightning and shadows can play tricks on a person," Ty said.

Last night she'd been so certain, but that was during the storm. Yet there was that light in the window and Partner had seen something that caused him to shy. Ty didn't believe her. No big surprise. It did sound silly.

Putting his boot into the stirrup, Ty mounted Joker. "You saw Image right here last night?"

"Uh huh, right here, but I have no idea where he is now. Where are you going?"

"To find your goofy horse."

After one unsuccessful try, Heather swung onto Partner.

"There's an old barn and outbuildings over there. I'm assuming even that horse of yours has the brains to get in out of a storm."

Heather circled wide around Charlie's cabin. Partner seemed at ease now. Maybe she had been imagining things last night.

The buildings near Charlie's place still looked fairly sturdy, considering their age. A high pole fence bordered one structure, which Heather took for the barn. The corral gate hung open on its hinges and Ty and Heather rode their horses through. They headed into the barn, which was minus one door. A rustle in the corner caught their attention.

Curling his fingers, Ty blew on his nails then polished them on the front of his shirt. "Am I a genius or what?" He nodded to where Image stood, helping himself to a mouthful of hay from an abandoned manger.

Heather let out a relieved sigh. "Do you think he's all right?" She slipped from Partner and walked forward, holding out her hand to the Thoroughbred.

When Image bolted, Ty's rope settled over the big horse's head and tightened around his neck. The gelding seemed so surprised, he almost sat down.

"Horse," Ty said, "you've got a lot to learn."

"Thanks," Heather said.

"It's the least I can do seeing it was all my fault." He winked.

Heather couldn't look away from Ty's kind, brown eyes. "It wasn't anyone's fault."

He grinned. "Really?" He stepped off Joker who backed up, keeping the rope tight as if Image had been a calf. Ty took the halter from his saddle and put it on Image. Then he attached the lead rope and slipped his lariat off the gelding.

"Your horse, Milady." Ty swept his hat from his head in a bow. "Do you want him, or shall Joker and I struggle along?"

Heather giggled. "Would you mind?"

"Yes, but I'll do it anyway."

"My hero."

"Don't you forget it."

"Thanks, Ty. Thanks for everything."

"All in a day's work."

After coiling his lariat, Ty secured Image to the saddlehorn. He legged Heather up onto Partner and they rode out of the barn. Image trailed along behind Joker.

Another day Heather might have reveled in the smell of the fresh, clean air after the rain and the splendor of the mountains that stretched into the enormous blue sky. But this morning as she followed Ty and her wayward horse through the corral and out into the sagebrush, her gaze riveted on the house that had already caused her so much worry.

"Remember old Charlie? You know, the man we were talking about at dinner the other night?" Ty had probably noted the direction of her stare. "That's where he killed himself."

He paused, watching for a moment, then said, "I don't think Dad likes us messing around here for some reason, but should we check it out?" A mischievous grin played upon his face.

Heather hung back. "Won't we get in trouble?"

Ty lifted his hat and scratched his brow with the back of his wrist. "Shoot, why should he care? We won't hurt anything and I've always wanted to see where Charlie did it."

After securing the horses to a nearby pine, Ty sauntered across the rickety porch and reaching for the knob on the door, he turned. "Coming?" He held out his hand for Heather who still stood beside the horses.

Not wanting to appear overly wimpy, she crept forward. With Ty here, she hoped to put this whole Charlie business out of her mind. She took hold of his hand as they stepped through the unlocked cabin door.

At first everything looked pretty much as she remembered it—dusty, faded. But then she experienced how it felt to have her flesh crawl. There on the floor and splattered up the wall was a dark red stain. Her dinner from the night before rose in her throat. "Is that what I think it is?"

"My gosh, I don't know. Kinda looks like it, doesn't it? They said he died in this room." Ty stooped for a closer inspection. "Seems funny it would appear so fresh after all these years."

Heather couldn't focus her eyes. That blood was fresh. No way could it have been here when she and Katie visited weeks before.

"They said part of his brains were stuck on the wall. I don't see any brains, do you?" Ty asked.

Putting her hand over her mouth, Heather raced through the door. Ty followed at a respectable distance.

CHAPTER TWELVE

Heather lay watching the early morning, mid-July sunlight filter through the trees outside her window, forming patterns on the bedroom's worn carpet. The strange happenings at Charlie's still baffled her. She'd tried to forget about the missing painting, the sound of dragging chains, that . . . that thing she'd seen, and the . . . she shivered, the blood, but— nothin' doing. Her mind refused to cooperate. She liked these people. Whatever bothered them concerned her. Besides, curiosity had kicked her brain's wonder process into high gear. Hopefully this curiosity wouldn't kill the cat—or the nosy city girl.

"I'm almost up," she called, hearing tapping at the door. Cattle drive today—a real one, not merely herding a few cows. This one was more like three hundred.

"Just checking," said a voice she recognized as Ty's. "The dogies are waiting."

By six A.M. Heather had been stuffed full of hotcakes, entertained by watching Colton—handsome as ever in a faded Levi jacket and worn jeans—and hurried off by Bea to the barn along with Ty, Colton, Katie and Wells to tack up their horses.

Image's disposition had improved little during the night. He lifted his head out of Heather's reach as she tried to bridle him. Determined to win this new battle, she looked for something to stand on. She eased onto the edge of the straight stall manger and leaned out, bridle in hand. He sidestepped, swung his head and sent her tumbling. She grabbed only air and was fishing herself out of the hay-filled manger, amidst torrents of laughter from Katie, when Dallas Taggert arrived.

Heather had formed a mental picture of what this man Ty and Katie seemed hesitant to call their uncle might look like. No way could she have prepared herself for that moment Dallas barged in through the barn door. Jake, the ever-faithful cow dog, yelped as the big man stomped across a puny paw.

"When are you going to do away with this worthless animal?" he asked his younger brother, Wells. "You and I both know he's outlived his usefulness."

Katie plucked hay from Heather's hair. "That's what we've been saying about Dallas for years," the redhead whispered.

Heather rubbed her chin. Maybe Katie felt as she did that Dallas could have avoided stepping on Jake's paw. She peered up, way up, to study Dallas's face and focused on a rougher, larger version of Wells, but the wrinkles around his mouth turned down.

"It's good to see you too," Wells returned, stooping to pat Jake's head.

"A little grumpy today are we, Uncle Dallas?" Katie asked.

His nostrils flared. "Better get your mom to feed you better, Kate. Before I saw the red hair, I thought you were Ty."

Katie blinked and Heather's jaw dropped. For rude. True, her friend could stand some filling out, and with braces and frizzy red hair, she wasn't someone who'd turn David's head, but then who was these days?

A part of Heather still ached to hear from him, but looking forward to times like today—out in the fresh air, riding a good . . . uh, tolerable horse, watching two great-looking guys act macho—would help soothe the pain. She'd survive and so would Katie. Someday her friend would grow out of her pollywog stage and show everybody. Her own mom had said Heather would. Her mouth twisted. Darn. When?

"Got my horse ready?" Dallas asked Ty, who stood quietly adjusting the cinch of a chunky gray gelding.

From under the brim of his hat, Ty replied, "He's a bit edgy since he killed the groom last week, but you can handle him . . . no doubt."

Dallas stepped back and cast Ty a pained look.

So this explained why there'd been no good-natured kidding at breakfast. Only Colton had seemed himself. He greeted his uncle with a broad grin.

"Colton, my boy," Dallas said, the set of his granite-like jaw softening into a smile. "Everything's ready for your check ride on Friday. Come down early and we'll run through a few things beforehand." He patted this nephew on the shoulder.

All at once Heather felt like a bug in a bottle. Dallas's black eyes seemed to bore into her soul. She brushed hay from her jeans.

"The cowboys are getting prettier." He poked Colton. "Now I see what's been keeping you up here."

"This is Heather," Colton said, "our friend from Utah."

The man's smooth hand shot out—no calluses here. "Pleased to meet you, I'm sure." Not even his wide grin and fairly handsome face could make her forget his comment about Katie or stepping on Jake's paw, perhaps not by accident.

"Here," Ty said, leading the gray between Heather and his uncle. "Are we going to get those cattle moving or stand here all day jawing?" He fetched Image's bridle from the manger and, with only minor objections, slipped it onto the horse's head. He tossed the saddle over the gelding's back and cinched it tight.

Driving cattle proved more difficult than how it was shown in the movies. The obstinate critters seemed to delight in stampeding down hillsides or disappearing into inconvenient places. The calves, cute little devils, with soft, curly hair and tiny feet, had to be watched carefully or they'd turn back, and as Ty had put it, "encourage mom and the girls to do the same and then there's heck to pay." That's where Jake came in. He darted back and forth behind the cattle barking and biting backs of legs. Could this be the dog Dallas suggested had outlived his usefulness?

While Colton, Dallas, Wells and Jake circled the main herd of close to one hundred, Heather, Ty and Katie combed hilltops and gullies for strays. At the sight of an unusually large cow, Image leaped high enough to clear any show ring obstacle. Only luck and a fortunate grab for the mane kept Heather astride. She got to thinking that perhaps she and her horse were more hindrance than help, but nobody said anything.

As the drive progressed, she noted Colton scarcely left his uncle's side, and his expression when he looked at Dallas seemed a lot like Jake's when he watched Wells.

Once, while Ty searched for evaders, Katie and Heather drove a calf and four pairs toward the main herd. Colton sat with one leg slung over the saddle horn visiting with Dallas. Below in a gorge where the main herd had settled, Wells and Jake kept careful watch.

On his horse apart from the others, with only a dog for company, Wells appeared so lonely.

"Colton and his uncle sure seem close, " Heather said.

"Yeah," Katie returned. "Dallas stole Colton from Dad."

Heather kicked Image across a trickling stream. "What's that?"

"Ever since Dallas lost his son, he's done everything he could to weasel in on Colton." She glared at a cow as if daring her to head in the wrong direction.

"Dallas had a son?"

"Not for long," Katie returned. "Both Aunt Eve and the baby died when he was born."

"How awful," Heather cried. She could see now why Dallas might reach out to Colton. Maybe she'd judged the man too harshly. Everyone needed someone. She frowned. Who did she have now that Kevin and her mother were so wrapped up in each other and the new baby? David too probably dated some new darling at college.

"Even though Dad says he and Dallas never cared much for each other," Katie continued, "Dad tried to help him. He didn't mind sharing at first, but Dallas doesn't share. By the time Dad realized what was happening, Colton was gone. You can see where his loyalties are now." She nodded toward her brother and their uncle who seemed to be enjoying a private joke. The boy's head tipped back in a hearty laugh. Heather knew those beautiful green eyes of his would be sparkling.

The cattle the girls had rounded up saw the main herd and moved along easily, giving Heather a chance from this higher vantage point to appreciate the beauty around her. The unspoiled vastness appealed to her most—well almost. Throughout the day other scenery had vied for her attention.

Colton sat a horse nearly as impressively as Ty. The muscles flexing in their legs beneath form-fitting jeans, their handsome suntanned faces, the hair brushing over their collars hadn't escaped her notice. All this and sprawling rangelands of prairie grass and sagebrush that stretched to the base of pine-covered mountains.

She and Katie rode along that base now, mountains rising on one side while meadows spread out below.

"Didn't your uncle ever remarry?" Heather looked back at Katie.

"Nope. I hear tell there was someone a long time ago, but no one knew much about it. He's all flirt anyway, like Colton." She flashed Heather a sidelong glance.

Feeling color crawl up her cheeks, Heather tried to remain cool, but she understood. Colton wasn't interested in her. No boy could be for long. She always did or said something stupid. Like the other night. What a sight she must have been in her bright red pajamas.

Hoofbeats sounded behind her and Heather turned to see Ty driving two cows and a calf. He flashed her a grin. "You're a good rider. I don't know how you stick that English saddle. I couldn't."

"Thanks," Heather called as he rode by. Why couldn't every guy be as easy to get along with as Ty? With him she didn't have to worry about doing something dumb. Whoever said a guy couldn't be a girl's best friend?

Heather shook her head and let the breeze blow through her long hair, which turned browner daily from the roots out. The air carried a scent of sagebrush and cattle, along with a hint of peppermint. She felt a freedom she had never before experienced.

Image must have sensed it too. The bow came out of his back and he began to obey commands without objection. Her spirits soared. How great to be alive. Home seemed far away and with it the feeling of rejection and inability to measure up.

At last the cattle were gathered into one big sea of brown, black and white. Most were white-faced Herefords, but there were also the smaller Black Angus and a combination of the two. Charolais bulls were responsible for the off-color cattle that would every so often catch Heather's eye and remind her of the pure white cow she'd seen at Charlie's. Ty had explained that because of their ability to produce huge calves, the pure white Charolais bulls were his father's attempt to improve the herd. From the looks of the large, light-colored calves, it was working. Of course, Dallas, Katie had said, had been against the idea from the start.

As the hours passed, Heather wondered if they would ever transport this squirming mass of bawling beefsteak through, around and past all the places they didn't want to go.

"How's your rear?" Ty asked, riding by Heather again. Even though she was certain her tailbone had penetrated clear through her skin, she merely rolled her eyes.

"I think we're about there. Oh, guess what?" Ty said. "I just overheard Dallas telling Colton about a murderer who escaped from the prison in Deer Lodge night before last."

"Really? Is Deer Lodge far from here?"

"About a hundred miles. The guy's probably heading straight for Canada," Ty returned before spurring his chestnut mare forward.

Wells rode ahead to open a gate while Heather and the others brought the cattle along slowly. One cow sauntered through the opening and the others poured through, then fanned out onto the rich mountain pasture like a river joining an ocean.

Following the cattle through, Heather noticed that Wells sat quietly upon his horse, as though hypnotized. He stared into the valley below. Heather's gaze followed his and she drew a quick breath. From this angle, Charlie's ranch seemed to leap out from its surroundings.

How odd that circumstances continually placed Heather near this mysterious property. But maybe not. The Taggerts had recently purchased the land, so naturally they'd go there more often. Had Katie known the drive would take them near Charlie's ranch?

While Heather watched, Dallas joined Wells and they spoke in low tones. Heather couldn't make out much of the conversation, but she thought she heard Dallas say the word, "prism."

Wells mumbled something like, "protecting yourself."

Ty, Katie and Colton brought a few stragglers through the gate. Colton rode up beside Wells and Dallas and the conversation ended abruptly.

Ty closed the gate.

Katie found Heather and whispered, "Did you notice where we are? I wonder if Charlie's still around."

Remembering the blood-stained floor, Heather forced a laugh. "Nah. He's probably gone off to a ghost convention or something."

CHAPTER THIRTEEN

What had Wells and Dallas been discussing that involved a prism? Prism. Hmm. Prism, or was it, Heather shuddered, prison? Was there something more than Colton's loyalty that had caused hard feelings between these brothers?

Glad for a chance to think about something besides Wells and Dallas's conversation and their nearness to Charlie's place, Heather rested on a fallen tree trunk between Katie and Ty to eat the lunch Bea had prepared. The sandwiches packed in Partner's saddlebags looked delicious. After five hours on horseback, Heather felt like she could, as Ty had put it once, "eat the south end of a northbound skunk."

She peeked between the slices of homemade bread. Whew. Peanut butter and jam. No meat. Good. Watching these darling little calves had almost made a vegetarian out of her.

Oranges and chocolate chip cookies wrapped in Ty's jacket and tied onto the back of the saddle completed the meal.

"It's so beautiful." Heather studied the tall grass rippling in the breeze against the legs of their tethered horses like waves in a green sea.

Ty pushed his hat back. A curl popped out from under its covering. His hair was growing back to its pre-haircut length.

"I've always loved this area," he said. "Charlie's dad knew what he was doing when he bought this place. It's near perfect—has its own spring, good fences—or at least they were once. They need some fixin' up now."

"Because," Katie held up a finger, "without good fences you can't run cow one." She grinned at her brother.

"You listened." He reached around Heather to give Katie a shove.

Heather's flesh tingled at the touch of his arm against her back. She cocked her head.

"You know I always listen to you." Katie batted her lashes.

"Yeah, yeah. Sure you do." Ty took off his hat, combed his fingers through his hair, then fitted the hat back on his head. "Hey, look, Heather. There's the barn where we found Image and the outbuildings and house. You know, that place is still pretty decent."

He tore a bite from his sandwich and chewed, still staring down the mountain. His canteen rested alongside his boot. Picking it up by the strap, he offered the girls some water.

Katie leaned away with a scowl. "Did you drink out of it?"

"Yeah. So?"

"Geez, gross. Germs! Don't touch it, Heather. Dad's got some. He'll let us drink first."

"I'll wipe it off." Ty's brow furrowed. "You'd think I had anthrax, or something."

Reaching for the canteen, Heather dropped the orange she'd just peeled on a baggie and smiled at Ty. "I'm not worried. Thanks." She took a couple of gulps then passed it to Katie.

She started to drink.

"It's got germs," Ty said.

"Well, Heather's are on top."

Ty stared at her blankly then shook his head.

Heather giggled.

"Know what?" he said.

"What?" Katie asked.

"I'm gonna ask Dad if I can fix up Charlie's house."

Katie coughed and glanced at Heather. "Dad's gonna tear it down."

"What? No way. Why?"

Ty turned to stare at Wells, as did Katie, then Heather. He and his horse still circled the herd. He kept his distance and Heather got the feeling he wanted to be by himself.

Dallas and Colton dismounted and tied their horses to fence posts about six away from Image and Partner. Colton touched the brim of his hat and smiled at Heather, then he and Dallas perched on adjoining rocks half a hillside away, retrieved their lunches from their saddlebags and began eating.

Heather felt a jab of disappointment that Colton chose Dallas instead of her as a lunch companion.

"Didn't you hear Dad talk about tearing it down the other night?" Katie went on. "Or maybe it was Colton who told me."

"I wonder if I can talk him out of it." Ty rubbed his chin. "You know, joining these two ranches will really make this property a going concern. We could live up here, if we wanted—get away from you know who."

"Wouldn't that be nice?"

"You'd like living up here?" Heather asked.

"Oh, I'd miss the other ranch, but . . ." Katie nodded in the direction of Dallas and her brother. "Look at those two—joined at the hip. They never give Dad a thought. Makes me want to barf."

Heather jumped when a voice said, "You sick, Katie?"

The girl swung her head around. "Oh! No, Dad. I didn't see . . . You move fast."

Wells plopped on the ground across from the three friends. "My big insides are eating my little ones," he said. "Anything left?"

"You bet." Katie dug into the saddlebags and pulled out a sandwich.

Ty handed him an orange and opened the bag of cookies, passing it around.

Cows and calves called back and forth as they located each other, sounding sort of like a really bad orchestra tuning up.

Had it not been for the jet trail slashing the blue of the sky, Heather would have thought she'd galloped back in time seventy years to when Charlie's dad still owned this place, before Charlie's death, before angry words between brothers.

"How do the mothers find the babies?" Heather asked Wells, still concerned about what he and Dallas could have been discussing.

"One of life's little mysteries." He stared off in the distance.

Speaking of mysteries, Heather thought.

"Believe it or not, the calves recognize their mother's call and vice versa," he continued, "also the smell."

"How long does it take for them to, what did you call it the other day, mother up?"

"Depends on the age of the calf, but with these I'd say about forty-five minutes to an hour."

Had Dallas really said "prison"? Did he mean Wells would be in prison? Ridiculous! He had to be one of the gentlest men she'd ever met. "Animals are amazing."

Wells didn't respond for a moment. He stared down the mountain in the direction of Charlie's. "Aren't they," he said finally and turned to watch Dallas and Colton finish their meal but not their conversation. It seemed they never ran out of things to discuss.

Having eaten, Ty jumped up. "I'll be right back."

"Looking for a tall bush?" Katie asked.

"Never mind. Just cuz you hold liquid like a camel."

"That's what you get for hoggin' the water."

Wells gulped down the sandwich and stuffed a cookie into his mouth. "I'm going to slip down and check those cows on the East Forty. Why don't the rest of you cut through the lease and head on home. I'll catch up later."

Katie sprang to her feet. "I'll go with you."

"No, Kate. You . . ."

"Where ya headin'?" Dallas said as he and Colton walked toward them, horses following.

"To check the cows on the Forty."

"We might as well all go," Dallas said.

Wells held his hand out as if to hold Dallas back. "No need for that. I'll be along shortly."

Dallas turned toward his horse, put his foot in the stirrup and tried to get on. The saddle slipped. He stepped down and tightened the cinch. With Colton holding onto the opposite side of the saddle to steady it, Dallas mounted. "I didn't know we had cattle on the Forty."

"There's a lot of things you think you know and don't," Wells returned, eyes flashing.

Heather pictured two bulls pawing the ground.

"Anyone need mosquito repellent?" Katie asked.

Wells turned, walked to his horse and swung on without using stirrups like Ty often did. The bay cantered down the hill. Charlie's cabin crouched in the distance.

Lifting one brow, Katie whispered to Heather. "Dad's actin' mighty strange. Do you think he's seen Charlie?"

After everything that had happened, Heather didn't know what to say, but, oh how she wished she could follow Wells. No way could she do that. It would make him mad and besides she'd already had a bellyful of that cabin. Then there was that little matter of needing to mind her own business.

"Do you think he did?" Katie asked again.

Heather shrugged.

All at once Image reared, fighting momentarily before the reins of his bridle snapped in two. She should have known better than to leave the excitable big horse tied with only his bridle reins. Image had never set much store in standing still and the mosquitos probably drove him wild.

The gelding started off at a trot, then began to canter.

"Here we go again," Heather said. "May I borrow Partner?"

"Need some help?" Dallas and Colton both asked.

"No. I'll probably be better off going by myself. Be right back."

Was she out of her mind? What a perfect opportunity to be alone with Colton. Actually, it was Ty she really needed, but he was nowhere to be seen.

By the time she'd untied and climbed on Partner, Image was long gone. Heather started off in the direction he'd taken. Perhaps he'd followed Wells's horse.

She found herself closer to Charlie's house than she wanted. Once more it seemed to glare at her. She moved some distance away, but even then remembered that thing she'd seen and felt like her nerves shot through her skin.

Suddenly the back of her neck tightened and a chill turned her cold. Out of the corner of her eye she'd noticed a slight movement near the house. Cautiously, she forced herself to look. What she saw startled her more than if the expected ghost had wavered there. It was Wells—Wells sneaking out of Charlie's house. He moved quickly as if he couldn't escape fast enough, his head turning from side to side.

Hoping not to reveal her presence, Heather urged Partner on.

Off in the distance she spotted Image grazing near a willow patch. On her way to get him, something else caught her attention beneath the low-hanging branches of a nearby cottonwood.

Heather saw a lone cow. Why was it so still? She drew closer. From a distance the animal had appeared to be asleep, but as she stood near, the cow still didn't move. Her head and neck curled around her body and her front legs were tucked up under a fat stomach. Lying here beneath the lofty cottonwood, she had sought an area of solace for the birth of her calf and eventually her own death. Heather wondered if the cow had seen her baby before she died. She noted there were no signs of the newborn, only of its birth. Heather blinked to clear her eyes.

When Ty, leading Image, found her, she still remained beside the cow. Hurriedly she brushed the tears from her face. Nobody cried at the death of a cow. But she'd never seen anything that large, dead before. She turned away. Silly girl. What must Ty think of her?

"Sad, isn't it," he said. "I always wonder what they were thinking just before they died. Animals have feelings too, you know. Don't let anyone tell you they don't."

All that Heather could muster was a quick nod. Ty could be so sweet.

Suddenly he exclaimed, "What the . . ." He edged behind the cow, moving aside a branch. "She's partially butchered. See?"

Now in a better position, Heather noticed that the cow's hind leg and part of her hip had been crudely hacked from her body.

"Dawdling again, huh, Ty?" Colton said. "Dad didn't go home like he planned. He came right back instead and sent me out to fetch you two. Boy, he's acting weird. So is Katie, but then with her how can you tell?" His eyes went from them to the cow. "Dang, another one? We can't afford much more of this. Dallas and I have been scouting around. Looks like we're missing about eight calves too." He snickered. "Maybe Kate's right. She thinks Charlie's come back from the grave and is up to his old tricks."

CHAPTER
FOURTEEN

Move your butt." Heather slipped between Image and the wall, pitchfork in hand. She'd cleaned out his stall yesterday, but working made her feel better. She wished she'd never heard the name "Charlie Phipps" or seen where he'd died. Maybe the house was haunted. How else could she explain the strange things that had happened?

The gelding cocked his back leg.

"Hey!" Heather slapped him on the rump. "No kicking." She stepped away, pointing the dangerous end of the pitchfork. "Don't tempt me. I'm in a mood."

Ty walked through the barn door, carrying a saddle across his arm. "You'd never hurt a horse, not even this one."

She pushed Image aside and scooped up soiled straw, tossing it into a wheelbarrow in the open gateway. "I'm pretending to be tough. It doesn't come naturally."

"Could've fooled me." Ty chuckled, moving closer. "Must be a stall-mucking mood."

"Excuse me?"

"You said you were in a mood." He tipped his head toward the wheelbarrow. "My room should be so clean."

"True. I've seen your room." She threw another moist offering into the wheelbarrow, barely missing Ty.

"Say! Not just mood, but attitude." He walked a short distance, swung the saddle onto a rickety wooden rack, then came back to lean on the gate.

"Sorry. Sometimes I'm not the best shot." She grinned, welcoming anything that would take her mind off Charlie . . . the missing painting . . . chains dragging . . . a butchered cow . . . And what had Wells seen that made him look so . . . so horrified when he came out of the cabin?

"Heather. Heather!" Ty waved his hand in front of her face.

"Huh? What?"

"Something bothering you?" He slid his hat back on his head, brows lifting.

If she didn't share her concerns with someone, the top of her skull would blow off. She'd thought about speaking to Katie, but that would be like holding a spark next to gasoline. She stood the pitchfork on its teeth and propped her hands on the handle. What she needed was a calm, sensible listener to convince her that Katie wasn't the only one whose imagination had ballooned to blimp proportions.

"What is it?" Ty touched her arm.

Heather started so speak, but no words came out.

Image stomped at a fly.

"What?" Ty asked, his brown Beagle eyes soft and accepting.

"You'll think I'm crazy." She leaned the pitchfork against the wall.

"I already do."

Her mouth fell open in mock despair.

"Just kidding. Go on. You can tell me."

"Promise. No matter what I say?"

"How bad could it be?"

"It's about Charlie."

His smile vanished. He stared at her blankly. "Go on."

"Strange things have been happening."

"Like what?"

Heather reviewed each event from the missing painting to the mutilated cow.

Ty rubbed his chin.

Moving toward the gate, Image stared out the barn door, ears pricked.

Heather's tale sounded so much like something Katie would say, she couldn't believe it and before she realized, she'd said too much. She hadn't meant to tell Ty about his father and uncle's conversation.

Image snorted.

"I think Dallas said something like 'prism' or . . . 'prison'." Heather swallowed. Too late she heard something outside.

Katie stormed into the barn. "I thought you were our friend," she snapped. "Don't you realize you're calling my father a murderer?"

"I am not. I'd never do that!" Heather reached for Image's mane, wanting something to hold onto. Did she really think Wells could kill someone?

"Why don't you leave? Everything was fine before you came." Katie whirled and charged out of the barn.

"I'd better go after her," Ty said, his face pale under the suntan. "No telling what she might do."

* * *

For two days Ty and Katie avoided Heather like slow death. Ty tried to be polite, but not Katie.

As in the past, whenever something bothered Heather she headed for the barn and her horse. She would have preferred Possum's comfort, but Image would have to do.

The muscles in the black gelding's neck quivered as she rode. Heather let the reins slip through her fingers. What did it matter? After botching things up so royally, did anything matter?

Image leaped a ditch, throwing Heather forward in the saddle. She pulled on the reins. His head came back, nearly striking her in the face. Still she tried to work out her thoughts.

Earlier that morning, Ty had suggested to his parents that he move into Charlie's house for the rest of the summer. Though Heather got the impression that his decision had something to do with her, like it or not, it seemed a workable plan.

"Shoot, Dad," he'd said. "I could fix up the old place while I watch after the cattle."

Katie looked as if she'd swallowed a slug.

"I don't want you around that awful house," Bea blurted.

Wells had put a comforting hand on his wife's arm, giving her a cautious glance. "No need for that, son," he said. "It'll be torn down soon."

Narrow-eyed, Ty had studied his father, then turned and toyed with the hotcakes on his plate. What was he thinking? Were his thoughts similar to hers?

Even though Heather hated herself for believing that Wells could be a murderer, she'd kept out of his way whenever possible and jumped when he entered a room unexpectedly.

Image galloped faster now. Wind whipped through her hair, sweeping it across her face when she turned her head. Normally Image's speed would have raised shivers along her spine, but not today. She welcomed it. She'd let him run. If she fell, so what? Wherever she went, she caused trouble—even at home. Kevin and her mother were happier without her. They hadn't written for a week and a half. Now she'd ruined her friendship with Ty and Katie. How could one person contaminate so many lives? She hadn't even had any real success with Image. Ty had encouraged her to jump the horse again, but she'd been too chicken.

At the opening of an eighty-acre field referred to as the "eighty" by the Taggerts, a gate stood with one side propped against a fence post. Sadly, Heather remembered how she'd joked with Ty on their last ride, telling him if he didn't hang the gate soon she'd haul it home to Kevin to use as a jump.

How easy it would be to maneuver Image toward that obstacle. Maybe he'd consider jumping now and she'd have one thing to be happy about. If not, it was only her neck at stake and who the heck cared? In fact, she almost hoped Image would miss the jump and send her crashing to the ground.

Heather pulled back on Image and pointed him at the gate. He fought the bit and cantered a step in place. Straightening out, he lengthened into his magnificent Thoroughbred stride and, without so much as a swish of his tail, sailed across.

"Ooh-eee," Heather yelled and opened her eyes. Her heart seemed stuck in her throat, but she grinned like a circus clown.

She drew the horse to a walk and stroked his glistening black neck. "You've been listening, haven't you? The ranch work and Ty's training suggestions are getting to you, in spite of your orneriness."

Thoughts of Ty made her insides cramp. He hated her now, no doubt about it. She should have given Wells the benefit of the doubt, no matter what.

Katie had told Heather to leave. Good suggestion. She'd caused enough trouble. How could she have suspected the worst of a kind, compassionate man like Wells? He'd been so wonderful to her. She'd head back and tell everyone she'd be going.

Image pranced toward the main ranch buildings. What was that up ahead? Heather shaded her eyes.

Barely able to stay in the saddle, someone swayed back and forth on a horse—Wells's horse, Duke. It was Wells, cradling an arm against his slumped body.

Heather kicked Image into a canter.

When Duke stopped in front of the barn, Wells teetered and fell to the ground.

Heather slowed Image and leaped off. She left the reins dragging. "Wells. Wells! What happened?"

She dropped to her knees in the dirt, turning him over. His blood-covered shirt stuck to his body and the silver buckle on his belt shone red.

"Gotta get that cow," he mumbled. "Rope. Where's my rope? Got tangled around my thumb. Took it clean off."

She took hold of his arm and pulled it away from his stomach. She swallowed her breakfast again. Only a bloody exposed bone remained where his thumb had been.

Her mouth went dry and her head spun. Don't you dare, she told herself. Wells needs you. Don't let him down again. She blinked several times and wiped her forehead with the back of her hand. Think! Oh how she wished she'd taken that Red Cross course they'd offered back home. What should she do? She jerked her belt off and wrapped it around his wrist, pulling it tight.

He struggled to stand. "Duke. Where's my horse? I hurt my thumb. Where's my thumb?"

Heather placed her hand on his shoulder, gently holding him down. "No. Don't stand," she told him, concerned that he made such little sense. "Sit here. Rest your back against the fence. Are you okay for a minute? I'll get help."

She whirled, started running, tripped over a rock and fell, scraped her hand, struggled to her feet and ran to the house. She flung the door open. It banged against the wall. "Bea, Ty, Katie! Help," she screamed.

No answer.

Bounding into the kitchen, she collided with Bea, sending a bowl and the potatoes she'd been peeling rolling across the floor.

"Sakes, child. What's the matter?" Bea took Heather by the shoulders. "Are you okay? Is that blood on your shirt?"

"Wells. He's hurt bad. His thumb's gone—just bone sticking out. Hurry, he's at the barn."

Bea grabbed a clean dish towel and held it under the faucet. She took ice from the freezer. Then they raced to where Heather had left Wells.

He sat with his back leaning against a fence post. His glanced up from the ground at his wife. "I hurt my thumb, Bea." He held up his injured hand.

"I see that you did. Here, let's wrap this around it." She spoke softly as if talking to a child. Heather marveled at the woman's composure. But when she turned to Heather, her eyes were wide and wild. "Find Ty," she said. "He's in the east field mending fences. Do you know where that is?"

"Yeah." Heather ran to Image and leaped into the saddle. Fortunately, he'd stayed by Duke instead of running off as she'd expected. "I'll get him." She kicked Image and he leaped in the air.

She gave the horse his head and his speed increased. His hooves made sharp pings as they struck stones in the road. Dust rose behind them.

Heather saw the gate to the entrance of the field where Ty would be fencing and pulled back. "Whoa," she screamed, see-sawing on Image's mouth. Normally she was much gentler, but today she had no choice.

Swinging down to open the gate, she saw Ty come bouncing along through the field in his pickup.

She waved her arms to motion him over. "Your dad's been hurt. You need to get him to the hospital. He's at the barn."

She opened the gate and Ty's truck sped off, flipping up clods of dirt.

He could have at least thanked me, she thought for an instant, then frowned. Sure he could have—thank the person who'd accused his father of murder, the father who now lay injured, needing his help. Not likely.

Closing and securing the gate, Heather struggled to climb back onto Image. Even after all the exertion, the horse wouldn't stand for her to mount. She hung halfway on as he started off in a trot. When she'd pulled herself completely astride, Heather caught a glimpse of Ty's pickup barreling down the dirt road now headed for town.

Duke whinnied when she and Image came into view. He still stood ground tied near the barn. Blood covered the front of the saddle and had dripped over his shoulders.

Water from the old pump next to the barn filled the bucket. Heather cleaned off dried blood from Duke and the saddle and sweat from Image then put both horses into stalls.

In the confusion of Wells's accident, no one had taken time to wonder about Katie.

CHAPTER FIFTEEN

Pulling aside the curtains in the Taggert front room, Heather peered out the window through branches of an old cottonwood tree, hoping to see lights in the barn. She shook her head and flung the drapes back in place. "Where is she?" It was almost dark and still Katie had not returned.

Heather paced and struggled to recall when she'd last seen her friend. At breakfast she'd asked Katie to pass the butter and received a cold stare. Then later that morning while saddling Image, she'd seen Katie ride off on Partner.

Suddenly Heather felt as if the air had been sucked from her lungs. She gasped, remembering. If only she hadn't been so caught up in her own problems earlier, maybe she'd have realized Katie rode toward the shortcut—the shortcut leading to Charlie's.

Lifting her sleeve, Heather glanced at her watch. Nine o'clock! When would Ty get back? Katie could be lying broken and bleeding somewhere. Heather couldn't just sit here. She had to do something. She'd never forgive herself if anything happened to Katie.

She scrawled a quick note and bolted for the door.

Image shuffled back and forth and when Heather pulled the cinch tight, he lay his ears back as if to say, "How dare you take me out again?"

"I know you're not real pleased about this, Mr. Beastie, and I'd ride someone else if I had a choice, but you and I both know everyone except Duke is out in the pasture. And since he's a stallion, even you might be better."

By the time Heather had Image saddled, it was 9:30. As she stepped out of the barn, she hoped to see Ty's truck. No such luck. Shivering, she passed the spot where Wells had sat looking so pale and weak. If Ty were still at the hospital, maybe his dad was worse than she'd thought. Wells just had to be all right, and so did Katie. Katie. Darn. Where was she?

Glad now that she'd decided to go after her friend, Heather knew it was the least she could do for the family who'd been so wonderful to her.

Finally she'd learned to mount this huge horse by herself thanks to hints from Ty. She'd find Katie for him, and for Bea and Wells. Katie had been pretty rude lately, but Heather had never stopped liking her.

Sticking the toe of her boot in the stirrup, she stretched up and grasped the leg roll of the English saddle, pulling herself up. Gathering her reins, she disappeared into the night, glad for the moon shining brightly above.

Compared to the city, the ranch had always seemed so quiet, but tonight she heard everything. As if they sensed her fear, the cattle bellowed and even the crickets chirped their warning. Image's hooves, hitting rocks as she rode over the mountain trail struck her frazzled nerves like lightning bolts. The moon cast long, angry shadows in the trees.

It seemed like hours before Heather recognized familiar landmarks that told her she was close to Charlie's. She felt as if she were being drawn into a huge web.

Then she saw it. Her blood froze. A light . . . coming from Charlie's house.

Heather's breath shortened to deep gasps. She wanted to race Image back to the safety of the Taggert Ranch. Surely Ty would be there by now and he'd know what to do.

The light in Charlie's window flickered, like it came from a fire or lantern. Was Katie in there?

In spite of the coolness of the night, sweat trickled down Heather's face. Her hands gripped the reins, but she didn't turn Image. Something told her Katie needed help.

Think! She tapped her finger on her chin. She'd lock Image in the corral next to the old barn so he wouldn't break his bridle and run off, then she'd sneak back and steal a look. Maybe Katie wasn't inside. She could have returned to the ranch and at this very moment be wondering where everyone was. Heather wouldn't have minded wasting all this worry and concern.

But when she turned Image into the corral, her heart stopped. Katie's horse, Partner, stood in the corner, head down, eyes dull. He nickered. Katie was here, in the house, and most certainly in trouble.

Thoughts ricocheted through Heather's mind. She'd be crazy to go in there alone, But what about Katie? Was she hurt? What if someone—or something—wouldn't let her leave? Heather gritted her teeth. She had no choice. She had to go in and find her friend.

Leaving Image in the corral with Partner, she crept across the grass and sagebrush surrounding the house. Every rapid thud of her heart signaled danger ahead. What would she find when she got inside? Had Katie fallen, hurting herself so she couldn't ride? Perhaps that was it.

Heather slipped around the rear of the house to where another, dimmer light shone from a back window. She'd check this out first.

A dusty, tattered curtain covered most of the glass, but Heather could still peek through. Her hand came to her mouth. She made out the figure of a man lying on the floor. No, not a man—a boy about her age. His hands and feet were bound, his mouth gagged. Blood oozed from a cut above one eye.

Searching for another window she dared peer into, Heather eased around the outside of the house.

What was that? Crying? Katie! At least her friend was alive.

"See this? Found it in the cushion. Where's the rest?" a deep voice yelled.

Katie sobbed hysterically. "I don't know! What money?"

The porch squeaked under Heather's weight. She almost passed out from fright. What did she think she was doing? She was no match for whatever was in there. Yet Katie needed her.

Drawing closer, Heather peeked in, looked up, then stared up higher. She screamed—a desperate, bloodcurdling cry. A hideous face glared down at her through the opposite side of the windowpane.

Backing up, Heather tripped and almost fell. She leaped off the porch and headed into the darkness toward the barn, running like she'd never done before. Something grabbed her by the hair.

She kicked and screamed. A vice-like grip closed around her throat. Her lungs fought for air. Dizziness overtook her.

"Quit squirming!" growled a voice. "You're pretty. Don't make me kill you."

When the tightness on her neck eased, she sunk her nails into hard flesh. A blow alongside her head brought fireworks to her eyes. Then her vision blurred and everything went black.

CHAPTER SIXTEEN

Heather's eyes felt like someone had packed them with sawdust. Blinking, she fought to adjust to the darkness surrounding her. She groaned and struggled to put a hand to her brow. Ropes bit into her wrists and ankles. "Oh no!" she whispered, panic tightening her throat. Thoughts of the horrible face and vicious blow brought a sob to her lips.

"I thought maybe you were dead," a voice said.

"Get away!" Heather screamed. "Don't hit me again!"

"It wasn't me!" he said.

She shivered and stared in the direction of the sound. "Who . . . who are you?"

Across the room, the floor squeaked. "Phipps," the voice said. "Not that it matters."

"Who?" her voice cracked. "Char . . . Charlie Phipps? You're dead." Her head ached and she felt something warm oozing around the back of her ear.

A weak laugh. "Not yet I'm not. Charlie Phipps was my dad. I'm Chuck. You just had to show up, didn't you? Now you're in as much trouble as me and that loud-mouthed kid in there."

Heather lifted her head from the cold, wood floor. "Is Katie okay?"

"She was. I expect she's as well off as you and me—at least for now."

Rolling over and bending her legs to the side, Heather wiggled into a sitting position. Her eyes adjusted to the night and she made out the shape of a figure a few feet away. Of course—the boy she'd seen earlier when she peeked in the window. She wished the lantern were still here. Shoot, she wished a lot of things, but for a minor wish, a light might have helped.

"What's going on?" Heather cried. "What does that maniac want?" A tear slid down her cheek.

"Search me," Chuck said. "He's been holding me here for three days. Well, I think it's been three days, anyway. He keeps asking about money. I found about seventy bucks stuffed between the cushions of that old couch in the other room. Now he thinks there's more. He's been tearing the place apart. He's a couple of screws short. You don't know anything about any money, do you?"

"Me? No. Of course, I'm a poor one to ask. I'm just visiting."

"Tough luck. Tough for all of us. I think the only thing keeping us alive is he figures one of us knows about that money—a lot of money from what I can tell. He even seems to think that's why what's-her-name—Katie—showed up."

What was that smell? Bile rose in Heather's throat. Yuck. Some dead animal or something, at least she hoped it was an animal.

She fought the ropes until her wrists stung, but the knots held. Her head cleared a little as anger mixed with fear. "Well, I'm not going to just . . . Can't we get out of here?"

"Oh, yeah, sure." He groaned and twisted, probably working on sitting up. "Believe me, I've tried. That's how I got this cut on my head. Now he only lets me loose once in a while to take a leak, eat some stale bread, or gulp a few sips of water. I don't know why he bothers. He's going to kill us anyway."

"Please don't say that." She swallowed the big lump in her throat. "How did you get in this mess?"

He snickered. "Don't think I haven't asked myself that a hundred times. I'm an idiot." He paused, coughed. "I thought it would help if I saw where they lived."

He sounded so forlorn and beaten, Heather couldn't help feeling sorry for him. Shoot! She felt sorry for them both—and Katie. Heather hadn't heard any sound from the girl since coming to.

Cocking her head, Heather listened intently, hoping to hear something from Katie, but any creak in the floor, any sign of light also meant that monster who'd hit her might be coming back. She gritted her teeth. "Who? Your parents?" she asked, fear not yet overshadowing curiosity.

"Yeah, well . . . my mom. I never knew Dad. He died before I was born." His voice trailed off for a moment, then he spoke again.

"I had a friend once," he said, "but mainly there was just Mom. I used to watch her at her easel. She painted this cowboy once. It was really good, maybe her best work. She burned it though. After that she did pictures of me, mostly. I guess I was all she had too."

Now that she'd stopped struggling, Heather found she could maneuver her wrists. The ropes weren't as tight on one arm as the other. "You loved her a lot."

"Yeah. After she died, I couldn't eat. Couldn't sleep. I just sat in my room and stared into space. Finally the guy we rented our place from told me I had to get out."

Heather heard Chuck rustling around. He worked himself over to the wall and leaned against it.

"Mom used to talk about this place," he went on, "not so much in the end, but when I was young. She never would bring me here, though. After she died, I didn't have anywhere else to go, so I thought I'd come and see if the house was still standing. I hitchhiked most of the way from Denver before I found a truck for a hundred dollars."

"No houses to haunt in Colorado?" Heather wriggled on the cold floor, trying to find a comfortable position. Blood still dribbled down her neck from the cut on her head.

"So you figured it out. That Taggert girl gave me the idea the first day you two showed up. She was so ready to believe. I thought maybe I could scare her off and have the place to myself. I didn't figure on so many of you showing up all the time. You kept me hopping, I tell you."

Heather rested her sore back against a rickety chest of drawers, the sole item of furniture in the darkened room except for a sagging bed and broken chair. "So you made all the noises—the dragging chains. You took the painting. Oh! Geez! You're who I saw that night in the rain. You frightened my horse. How come you looked so weird? I suppose you'd have left me there to die if I'd have been hurt real bad."

"No way. I didn't mean to frighten you. You freaked me out. It got real cold in the house during the storm and I'd gone out to find wood. I guess it was that old ski mask I found in the house that scared you. Sorry. Anyway, I stuck around watching until that boy, Ty, showed up."

Heather's heart stopped as she heard movement in the next room. Was it Katie, or HIM? She waited, expecting at any moment to see the giant's horrid face. When nothing happened, she continued in a lower tone. "Thanks for that anyway. But why did you do it, Chuck? The Taggerts would have let you look around, maybe even given you permission to stay. They're really nice people."

"I heard Katie say her dad didn't want anyone hanging around here."

Teeth chattering, Heather clamped her jaw shut. She wouldn't think about how cold she was—how afraid. She'd think about Chuck. He was right. Wells wouldn't have wanted a stranger here. She remembered how terrified he'd acted that day she saw him coming out of this house. Maybe, like her, he'd seen the blood or another one of Chuck's pranks. Did Wells have a guilty conscience? Is that why he'd gone to the cabin—to convince himself there were no clues left that could incriminate him?

She wouldn't think about that either. She'd clear up some of the other mysteries that had been plaguing her.

"Where did you get the blood, Chuck? I know it wasn't here that first day."

"From the calves," he said quietly. "I was surprised Ty didn't recognize it as fresh animal blood. He might have if you hadn't left in such a hurry."

"You've been killing calves? How could you?" Heather's arms ached from being tied behind her.

"Only the weak ones and sometimes they'd already died on their own. I got low on funds and supplies and since my old truck gave out on me, I had to eat something. A cow died once having a premature calf. I took part of the cow and the calf, but then the meat went bad and I couldn't catch anything else. Don't think I felt good about it. I've never killed anything before."

"Colton said there were a lot of calves missing. Did you kill all of them?"

He sighed.

"Well? You might as well spill it. Not too much worse can happen to you—or us. It helps to talk, don't you think?"

"I don't know. Maybe."

"Go on then."

"Well, okay." He leaned forward, stretching his shoulders. "When I first got here, I stumbled onto three teenagers rounding up calves and putting them into a horse trailer. They weren't too happy to see me and, of course, I didn't want them hanging around. They gave me fifty dollars to keep my mouth shut—like I was gonna tell anyone—and they promised not to squeal on me."

"Honor among thieves?"

"Okay. Okay."

"What did they want with the calves? They were too young to be without their mothers and they had brands." Heather glanced at the door and pulled at the ropes around her wrists.

"They picked out late-born calves that hadn't been branded yet. They got one calf, though, that had been ear-tagged. They said they had some milk cows who could raise the calves and then they'd sell them as yearlings."

"You helped those guys steal Taggert cattle! Didn't that bother you?"

"Of course. I'm not as bad as you think. But the Taggerts owed me after what they did to my folks."

"What . . . what did they do?" Heather asked, her voice shaking.

"Mom never would tell, but it had to be pretty bad. She always swore she'd never allow Taggerts on her land, and you know what else?"

Heather was afraid she did. She worried that Wells and Charlie had fought over Diana and it had led to Charlie's death. Surely Chuck didn't suspect that too. She drew in a deep breath. "What?"

"The painting in the other room, the one I saw you looking at that first day?"

"The one you stole?"

"I didn't steal it. I took it down to look at and didn't put it back. It was exactly like the one my mom painted—the one she destroyed. The man in the picture was Wells Taggert, wasn't it?"

"What makes you think so?" Heather wasn't sure why, but she didn't want to let on all she knew.

"I think so because my mother painted it and because she cried over the man in that picture. I think so because my full name is Charles Wells Phipps. What did Wells Taggert do to turn my mother against him?"

The pieces of the deadly puzzle were falling into place. There seemed no doubt about it now. Wells must have killed Charlie.

Light from the dawning sun filtered into the room through dirty windows and worn curtains. Heather saw Chuck more plainly now. Although he would have had to be at least nineteen, he was much smaller than either Ty or Colton and fence-post thin. Large, frightened, brown eyes stood out from his pasty white skin like pecans in fresh snow. His blond hair, matted with blood and dirt, was as filthy as his sweatshirt and jeans, evidence of what he must have suffered during the last three days. He looked vaguely familiar.

"We saw you at the Yesterday Café, didn't we?" Heather said.

He nodded. "I knew nobody would believe that ghost thing forever and decided to get out before things got heavy. I had enough money for one good meal before I left. Then you guys came in and it made me mad. Ty and Colton—they've got everything—money, friends, family. Right then I decided to stick around, maybe even tell the Taggerts who I was. On the way back here that night my truck quit and I've been on foot ever since. The old heap's still sitting on the side of a dirt road about five miles from here. Boy, how many times these last few days have I kicked myself for not leaving when I had the chance."

Heather lifted her chin. None of them deserved what was happening. Twisting against her ropes, she found that if she pulled real hard on her left hand she could work slack into the rope around the right. Blood pounded in her fingers. Clenching her jaw against the pain, she yanked with all her failing strength. Her skin tore, but her right hand slipped free.

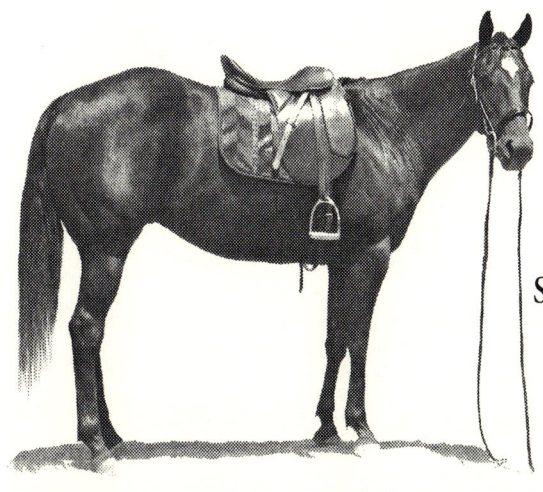

Heather struggled out of the ropes around her ankles. "How'd you do that?" Chuck asked. "I've been laboring for days."

"Don't know." Heather shook her head. "I have small hands. I guess he didn't think he'd need to tie a girl tight."

Chuck inched closer, scooting on his bottom. "Here, help me now."

She stumbled toward him, but stopped, lowering her head for the dizziness to clear. If only they could find Katie and make it to the horses.

Where was he? Where was that monster who'd hit her? Did he sleep or was he waiting outside the door ready to pounce?

Heather knelt by Chuck, her stiff fingers tugging at his ropes. "You think we can find . . ."

The door burst open. Screaming, Heather threw herself back, landing on the floor. She stared up in horror at a man whose bulk filled the entire doorframe.

A sneer spread across the giant's craggy face. His thick, dark beard only partially hid a jagged, red scar that descended from cheekbone to jaw. "Think you're smart, don't ya?" The matching shirt and pants seemed too small for his huge body.

"Leave us alone!" Heather yelled and felt the floor behind her for some sort of weapon—a stick, anything. Her fingers settled on an empty beer bottle. She struck it against the floor, hoping for a sharp edge.

The bottle bounced out of her hand.

"Now what ya gonna do?" He sprang forward and caught her by the arm.

She sank her teeth into his big fist.

He tore his hand from her mouth. Blood trickled from the wound. Striking her cheek, he sent her sprawling.

"Leave her alone!" Chuck shouted.

"She hurt me. Look what she did." The giant shoved his fist toward Chuck. The boy flinched.

Trembling, Heather spit on the floor. Her mouth still tasted of blood. She glared up at the big man.

His lip curled. Evil, dark eyes narrowed. Reaching down, he pulled her to her feet. The pressure around her wrist threatened to crush it.

"You're going to break my arm. Please don't. I'll be good," she whimpered.

As if her skin burned his, the man let go. His eyes took on a perplexed, glassed-over look. He backed away. "I don't want to hurt you, Ruby," he said almost gently. "I don't want to hurt anyone as pretty as you." He cocked his head. His fingers brushed her face as if he were afraid she'd disappear.

Heather stood still, not daring to take a breath.

He stared at her, then blinked several times as his eyes appeared to focus. "There was this girl once. She was pretty like you."

Heather rubbed her aching cheek. For a moment the man had been gentle. The giant had a weak spot. She was no match for his strength, but maybe, maybe she could . . . "I'd like to be your friend too, like her."

Too late, Heather realized her error.

"No!" the man yelled. "Not like her. She tricked me." He grabbed Heather by the shoulder and turned her toward Chuck. "Finish untying him, girl. Just his legs. No tricks. I don't like people who trick me." He squeezed her shoulder hard. "Understand?"

Chuck and Heather exchanged terrified stares as she obeyed. She pulled him up.

The man shoved Chuck through the door and nodded for Heather to follow. Every instinct told her to run, but meekly she did what she was told.

"In here," the man grumbled, taking hold of her arm. "We've got things to discuss."

The front room was not how Heather remembered. Rugs sprawled in a heap on the floor beside several couch cushions, their stuffing spilling out. Pale spots glared from soiled walls where pictures had once clung, and behind the stove, bricks had been pried from their mortar. Even a slab of wood beneath her foot had been torn from its resting place. Clearly the man had not found what he searched for.

Not knowing what to expect, Heather stood as if in a trance. Her eyes searched the room for some sign of Katie. She gasped. At the foot of the couch, hidden from view until now, a pair of motionless, bound legs protruded.

"Katie!" Heather screamed, pulling away from her captor.

He let her go. "She's all right for now, but if she doesn't put a muzzle on that mouth of hers . . ."

Heather knelt beside her friend, brushing red hair from a tear-stained face.

The younger girl's eyes shot open and she struggled to talk in spite of the piece of cloth binding her mouth.

"Everything's going to be okay, you'll . . ." Heather felt herself being thrown backward. She crashed against the battered couch.

With no sign of effort, the big man lifted Katie from the ground and dumped her on the couch along with Heather. He tore off her gag. "Now you'll tell me what I want to know." He took one braid in his huge hand and tugged. "Won't you?"

"Stop it," screamed Heather, then wished she hadn't.

"Shut up!" He turned his blazing black eyes on her.

Chuck moved in the doorway.

"Get over here, boy, where I can watch you," the giant said.

The three young people cowered on the couch. Only Heather held the man's stare.

He leaned back and folded his arms across his massive chest. "I'm gettin' tired of this. Are you going to tell me where my money is or do I have to beat it out of you?"

Chuck and Katie looked at Heather. They'd probably already told this man they knew nothing. What more could they say?

It was up to Heather now. Her mind raced.

Rising to her feet, she smiled at the big man. He'd seemed so childlike a moment ago. "I'm sorry I bit you. Here, let me see." She reached for his fist.

He stood still.

"Don't be afraid. I won't hurt you again." Taking his hand, Heather saw the ugly red teeth marks. She untied the scarf from her neck and tenderly wrapped it around the injury. "There. My name's Heather. What's yours?" She peered up into the man's hooded eyes and felt her stomach tighten.

The man shuffled from one foot to the other. "Pete—Pete Magleby."

She smiled at him again, her heart pounding so fast she thought she'd pass out. "Why do you think your money's here?" She fought to keep her voice even.

"Think?" Magleby shouted as Heather tried to swallow. "I don't think it's here. I know it is. I brought it here myself, and there's a heap more than that kid over there says he found. Why else would you all be hanging around this dump? What have you done with it?"

Careful, Heather warned herself. She pulled up the remains of an old chair, hoping it would hold Magleby's weight. "Sit down, Pete. May I call you Pete? If you tell me about it, maybe I can help. I'd like to help you. Come on, tell me about it."

Magleby studied her with laser-like intensity, but she didn't look away. Finally he said, "That scum Charlie said he'd keep the money safe until the hounds were away from the hole. He kept it safe all right. I did all the hard stuff and he kept the money, over $100,000. I counted it."

"That's a lie," Chuck cried. "My dad wouldn't do something like that. And besides, if he'd had any money, he wouldn't have left Mom and me without a cent."

Heather formed a shush with her lips, then turned back to Pete. "I know you're not lying. Tell Chuck where you got the money and why you brought it here."

Magleby peeked back and forth, like a child preparing to share a secret. A grin broke across his puffy face. "I stole it right from under the bank guys' noses." He chuckled. "Charlie told me how. He knew when there'd be lots of money in the bank and even what time the guard would be gone. Everyone says I'm dumb, but that guard was even dumber. He never even knew Charlie was pumping him for information. Him and Charlie were drinking buddies." Magleby leaned forward with his elbows on his knees.

Heather stood quietly, not wanting to disturb him.

"I dressed up like a janitor and slipped in when they were having a party. Just like Charlie said, no one even noticed. It was a whole day before they even knew the money was gone." He sat straight in the chair and lifted his chin. "Old Charlie was smart, that's for sure. He said we should hold tight—just hide the cash until things cooled down. At first he was nice, gave me jobs on his ranch. But after I had that trouble with Ruby and the law was searching for me, and I came back for my share of the money, Charlie called me dumb and told me to get out. He even pulled a gun. Nobody treats me like that. I'm tired of people calling me dumb." Magleby stomped one massive foot. "That guard in charge of the work crew at the prison called me dumb, but I showed him." He grinned wide, showing spaces where two teeth were missing. "It was his car I got away in. These are his clothes too. I left him tied up in his undies in a ditch." He paused, his eyes opening wide as if something had just occurred to him. "You don't think I'm dumb, do you?"

Nerves rubbed raw with tension, Heather jumped at his question. "You're not dumb, Pete," she returned, her mind still on what he'd been saying. "But how do you know Charlie didn't hide the money somewhere different after you left?"

The smile that crossed his face left Heather shivering as the icy gale of understanding swept over her.

"You killed my father," Chuck yelled and struggled to his feet.

"See, Heather, you were wrong about Dad," Katie whispered as if that were all that mattered.

Keep quiet, Heather wanted to scream.

Like a child transforming to demon, Magleby's face hardened. His dark eyes grew wide and fixed on Heather. He grabbed her by both arms and shook her.

Katie screamed.

Chuck lunged forward.

One hand still gripping his captive, Magleby swung at the boy with the other and sent him flying, then turned back to Heather.

"You tried to trick me. Now you'll pay. Just like Charlie. I didn't want to kill him, or my friend who was pretty like you. I could have gotten clean away after I killed her if Charlie would've given me my money. Those dummies at the prison, they never knew about Charlie, only about Ruby. His lips narrowed and he pulled Heather to him, his hands twisting in the lapels of her jacket. "I'll show you what I did to her."

Heather struggled to pull away. "No. Please don't. Don't hurt me," she whimpered.

Magleby tore her jacket from her, then reached for her shirt.

Hands still tied, Chuck threw his shoulder against Magleby, but another shove from the giant sent him sprawling into the sobbing Katie.

The front door burst open, crashing against the inside wall.

Ty charged into the room like an enraged stallion. He grabbed an old oak chair and smashed it across Magleby's head.

The blow would have brought most men to their knees, but this one merely shook his head and faced Ty, whom he outweighed by at least seventy-five pounds.

Ty delivered a punch to the big man's middle. Then one to his face. "Run, you guys," he yelled.

Magleby touched his face, brought his hand out and studied the blood on his palm.

Strangely, Heather thought of the day when the cow dog, Jake, battled the white cow. Her fingers froze as she tried to free Chuck from his ropes.

Ty made a play for Magleby's neck but hit short as the giant counter-punched. It caught the boy below the eye and opened up a gaping red gash.

Heather's breath rasped in her throat.

Swinging wildly, Ty tried to defend himself against the madman's crushing blows.

No contest.

Blood oozed from Ty's mouth and nose and he staggered.

Heather's head spun. Stars exploded and everything dimmed.

"Untie me, Heather," Katie screamed. "He's killing Ty."

Heather stared at the ropes but her fingers refused to move. It was as if she were somewhere else, another time, another place, as if she watched Jake protecting her from the enraged cow. In her mind she was running for the tree. Now she swung up into the branches. She watched as the cow whirled and kicked Jake in the ribs. The dog yelped in pain.

Like pressing rewind in her memory bank, Heather saw again the strange doorway leading into the ground.

The doorway! Of course, why hadn't she thought of it before?

The thud of a fist hitting flesh and Ty's groan brought Heather back to the present.

"Heather, please," Katie screamed.

Jumping to her feet, Heather flung herself between Ty and the madman. Now she felt she knew where Charlie had hidden the money.

She pounded Magleby's chest. "Stop it," she yelled. "Stop it and I'll tell you where the money is."

Magleby pushed her against Ty who swayed on unsteady feet. Heather caught him as he fell and both of them tumbled to the floor.

Picking up what was left of the chair, Magleby raised it above his head to finish Ty.

Heather sprang forward. "You'll have to kill me first. Then you'll never find your money. I know where it is." It was just a guess, a desperate ploy to save their lives.

Black eyes scrutinized Heather.

"I know where it is," she repeated, her voice steady.

Twisting her arm behind her, Magleby dragged her to the crumpled Ty. With his boot, he rolled the boy over.

Katie sobbed hysterically.

Ty lay still, eyes closed.

"If you're lying, I'll kill you," Magleby said and jerked up on Heather's arm. "If you're not, maybe I'll take you with me. You'll like me after a while."

CHAPTER EIGHTEEN

Magleby half shoved, half followed Heather out of Charlie's house. With a flutter of wings, a magpie flew up in their path. Strangely, she wondered if it was the same one she'd earlier freed from Charlie's house. She watched the bird soar in the sky, wishing she had wings. Her knees almost gave out. Was she living the last moments of her life? Even if they found the money, she doubted she would ever see her family again. If only she'd been better to them—not acted like a spoiled child just because her mom and stepfather were engrossed in their baby. Who wouldn't be? And what about Ty, lying in the house, maybe dead, and Katie? Wells? She'd wronged so many people. Her lungs labored as if they'd been tightly wrapped in cellophane.

As they reached the stairway leading into the ground, Magleby stopped short. His grip tightened on Heather's arm and his cruel eyes narrowed.

Then he looked at her with dawning understanding. "You really do know," he said.

He dragged her down the rickety stairs. She tripped on a fallen plank. Exposed roots of sagebrush and other foliage scratched her face as she caught herself against the damp chill of the earth. Entering this cellar was like descending into a grave.

A heavy wooden door with a rusty padlock stood at the bottom of the stairs. Taking hold of the lock, Magleby shook it and cursed. Though some screws of the supporting staple moved as he twisted it, the lock held.

Magleby, half-snarling, yanked Heather back up the stairway to where the plank that had caused her to stumble still lay. He picked up the heavy piece of wood.

"No! Don't!" she screamed, holding up her arm as a shield.

Magleby's face twisted into a leer. He dragged her back down.

Splinters flew in every direction as the door took a beating. At last the lock tumbled to the ground.

A musty smell wafted out of the frigid, dark interior. Spiders and sow bugs on the doorjamb scurried to hide from the alien light. Squealing, Heather brushed some creature off her shoulder.

Still grasping her arm, Magleby edged through the entrance, bumping his head and swearing again. The glow from the flashlight he'd probably taken from Katie illuminated the inside of the enclosure.

It reminded Heather of an old mining shaft, except for where certain logs had rotted through and earth had leaked in to reclaim the space. Large wooden bins stood against the sides of the space and upon the dirt floor.

Silent and cold, the room reflected only the meager light Magleby held in his hand. The walls seemed to close in on Heather as she stumbled after a man who had already taken two lives, and maybe . . . Her eyes clouded with tears as she thought of Ty lying in his own blood on the floor of Charlie's cabin. She prayed he hadn't been Magleby's latest victim, but then, maybe for Ty, the suffering was over.

The big man clutched her tighter. "Where's the money, girl?"

She stammered the first thing that popped into her mind. "Back there. Just keep going."

Suddenly the light in Magleby's hand stopped moving, then retraced its path to a section of log protruding from the rest of the wall.

He shoved fat fingers into a crack above the log and pulled. Heather watched as the piece of wood tumbled to the ground, realizing for the first time that he no longer held her. Already one hand deeply explored the gap where the log had been while the other fumbled with the light.

Heather glanced behind her. The door seemed miles away. She eased one foot back and almost fainted when the giant moved.

He propped the flashlight against the opening as both hands probed the hole. He couldn't seem to reach whatever had caught his attention. Rocks and dirt fell away as he worked.

Eyes never leaving her captor, Heather stepped backward.

His arms, hidden to the elbows, inched out of the hole.

As Magleby pulled a rusty metal box from its hiding place, Heather took another step back, then another. Her heart pounded so wildly she could barely breathe.

It seemed like an eternity before she reached the doorway. She saw Magleby open the box and heard his laugh. She shoved the door closed. Oh, no! She'd forgotten the lock was broken. Her sides heaving, she searched for something to block the door. The plank. A sliver embedded itself in her finger as she forced the big piece of wood into the space between the door and the bottom of the stairway.

Magleby pounded on the door. "You're gonna get it when I get out of here!"

Heather stumbled up the stairs and glanced in the direction of the corral where she hoped Partner and Image still waited.

Running back to Charlie's house, she wondered briefly how Ty had come. She couldn't see his truck. He'd probably ridden one of his horses in hopes of finding her or Katie on the return trail.

Thoughts of Ty and the others brought renewed speed to her faltering footsteps. How could she stand it if he died?

Katie and Chuck stared up with huge, terror-filled eyes when she charged in through the front door. Hands still tied behind their backs, they knelt beside a motionless, bloodied Ty.

"He's not . . . He's not dead, is he?" Heather's voice shook.

"He's alive," Katie said, "but I don't know for how long. He's hurt real bad."

Ty, alive! For a second, nothing else mattered. Strength flowed through Heather's body. "We've only got a second. Come on!" She stooped, untied Chuck, then Katie. "Chuck, help me with him. Now!"

Ty groaned as Heather, Chuck and Katie struggled to move him. Blood dripped from his mouth.

Chuck and Heather staggered out of Charlie's house, Ty draped between them. Katie hurried ahead in search of the horses. Heather glanced toward the root cellar, expecting Magleby's ugly mass to emerge any moment.

Ty's weight increased upon her shoulders as his head drooped. They stumbled forward. "Hang on, Ty," she pleaded. She ignored the pain in her back and the dizziness blurring her eyes. Blood oozed down her neck. Exertion must have opened her wound again.

Katie ran toward them, leading Partner. "I couldn't catch the others," she shouted.

Somehow they lifted Ty onto Partner's back. The boy slumped over the saddlehorn, teetering.

"Chuck, climb on behind Ty," Heather cried. "You're the strongest. Get going that way." She gestured. "Partner knows where. We'll catch up."

As she and Katie raced to the corral, Partner started off with Chuck steadying Ty.

Flipping foam from his mouth, Ty's gray gelding charged around the corral. Image lunged forward, rearing when his reins tangled around a post. Heather dragged her bruised body over the six-foot fence and groaned. Arms outstretched and waving wildly, she cornered and caught Sage. Katie labored with the gate she'd had the presence of mind to shut after leading Partner out.

"Here, Katie, climb on. I'll get Image." Heather boosted her friend onto the prancing gelding.

Image had worked his reins into a groove between post and pole. Heather battled to free him. "Whoa, boy. Easy." She struggled to keep her voice calm.

Katie screamed—a horrible cry that chilled Heather's blood.

Her hands clutching the now free reins, Heather spun around. Magleby's massive form blocked the open gateway.

Heather gasped and searched for Katie. The girl sat motionless on Ty's gelding, who pranced in place.

"Go Katie. I'll follow," Heather yelled, jolting her frightened companion into action. Katie brought the reins down hard on the gray's rump and he bolted past Magleby, knocking the big man aside.

He turned and watched Katie go, then riveted his black eyes on Heather. His lip lifted into an evil curl. "You tricked me. Just like the others." He pulled the gate closed. "Now I'll have to kill you."

Like a mouse in a grain barrel, Heather saw no escape. Still she swung into the saddle.

Image reared, striking out with his front legs. She barely kept her seat.

"Heather," Katie screamed from outside the fence.

"Get out of here," Heather yelled. "You can't help me."

"No!"

"Get. I mean it. Ty needs you."

Heather heard hooves striking against rocks as they clattered into the distance.

"Give up, girl," Magleby snickered. "You can't get away." Hand outstretched, he moved toward them. Twice Image slipped past. Heather jerked her pant leg out of the giant's grip.

Running now, Image lay his ears flat against his neck. He seemed to fear Magleby as much as Heather did. Her mind ricocheting, she searched for a way out, knowing full well there was none.

Magleby moved with surprising ease in spite of his size. "You're ticking me off," he said. Whenever Image slowed, the giant drew closer.

The gelding fought for his head. The reins slipped through Heather's fingers and she buried her hands in his long black mane. Soon it would be over. Image couldn't canter in circles forever. Suddenly he whirled and headed straight for the huge pole fence.

Heather closed her eyes. Visions of Image's finely carved legs mangled in the poles brought a lump to her throat. She tugged on the reins.

He snorted and pulled at the bit. He'd made up his mind. Now she had to. Well, okay—if the big horse felt he could do it, she'd darn well better help.

Image gathered for the jump and, leaning into his neck, Heather tightened her legs. They rose higher and higher. She waited for the sound of splintering wood—and bones. None came.

The fence stood behind them. Heather squealed.

Dropping her arms around the gelding's sweaty neck, she hugged him. Tears of respect and gratitude trickled down her cheeks.

Image lengthened his stride. Magleby could never catch them now.

Thanks to her horse, she'd escaped certain death.

But what about Ty?

CHAPTER
NINETEEN

Wind whipped past Heather and tugged at the dried blood plastering hair against her cheek. Wincing, she remembered the gash above her ear where Magleby had struck her. Somewhere out there Ty hurt too, only much more. Heather wondered why she hadn't caught up with the others.

Image's pace slowed as the incline of the hill increased and, not knowing which direction to take, she pulled the black gelding to a stop. He stood like a statue on the rocky knoll, his head high and ears pricked. He whinnied, then stood quietly as if, like Heather, he listened for any sound of his friend, Partner. The silence unnerved Heather and she jumped at the shriek of a hawk.

Shielding her eyes against the morning sun with her hand, she searched the landscape. Where were they? Perhaps Katie had decided the shortcut over the mountains would get Ty to help faster, or that Magleby would be less likely to find them on that route. But with Ty so badly injured, Heather wondered if Katie would have risked the more difficult terrain. Yet had they taken the easier path down toward the dirt road, Heather should've been able to see them from here.

"Katie!" she called. Her voice died off in a sob.

Her stomach twisted and a feeling of nausea swept over her. Suppose Magleby had found them and even now lay in wait for her? She clenched her teeth. That couldn't have happened—could it?

At the sound of rustling bushes and the crack of metal hitting rock, Heather swung around. The back of her neck tingled.

"Thank goodness it's you," Chuck called as he trotted Partner from behind a cluster of rocks and pines. "You got away."

"Yeah." Heather's voice came out high. "Where's Ty?"

Chuck motioned over his shoulder. "Back there in the trees. He's pretty bad."

She pressed her heels to Image. "Show me."

They trotted their horses for several minutes. Chuck led her over a ravine into a grove of pines. Ty lay near a huge rock.

Leaping off Image, Heather barely took time to loop his reins over a limb. She knelt beside Ty. Katie's jacket cushioned his head.

The girl held a piece of cloth torn from her shirt to his bloody, swollen cheek. Tears streaked her face.

"Oh, Heather, what can we do? He's so hurt."

Heather's throat tightened. She reached for Ty's hand. His fingers bent around hers and he opened his eyes.

"About time you showed up," he whispered. Using her hand to pull himself up, he struggled to sit. He'd started to turn light blue around his lips. "Where's the big guy? How'd you get away?" He began coughing.

Gently, Heather and Katie laid him back down. "Tell me," he said. "It helps take my mind off . . ."

Fighting back sobs, Heather removed her jacket and tucked it around Ty. "Magleby's got the money now. He's probably hightailing it cross-country. I hate to think what he planned for me, but Image jumped the fence and we got away."

"That huge corral fence?" He sounded hoarse.

"Yeah. And Ty . . ." She touched his arm. "I guess Katie told you Magleby killed Charlie. I don't know how I could have thought your dad did it. Can you ever forgive me?"

"No need. I wondered too." He choked—coughed up blood.

"Ty!" Katie cried.

The boy's eyes closed.

Heather's hand shook as she felt for a pulse in his neck. "He must have passed out. Someone's got to get to the ranch. If no one's there, at least bring back Ty's truck."

Chuck had kept his distance, but now he led Partner forward. "Let me go. You two should be with Ty."

"You don't know the way," Katie said. "Heather, will you go? Image is the fastest."

Heather wiped her face with the back of her hand. She hated leaving but knew Katie was right.

After what she hoped would not be her last look at Ty alive, Heather climbed onto Image. She'd already decided to take the faster route over the mountains. She raised her hand in parting and reined her horse around.

He started off, then began to buck. But for the first time since Heather had been riding him, he didn't scare her. She tightened her reins and kicked him hard in the sides.

With a toss of his head, Image leaped forward. Heather's legs held her like a vice upon his back. He snorted, then broke into a canter.

A slight smile touched her lips. She'd won. They headed at top speed toward the mountain pass. Each tick of the clock robbed

Ty of his dwindling strength. The thought that he might die filled Heather with a dread she could have never imagined.

As she reached the point where she'd begin her ascent over the pass, something below caught her attention. A cloud of dust filtered its way into the cloudless sky. She pulled Image to a stop and squinted. A vehicle traveled fast along the dirt road below.

Whirling Image around, she bent her body against the racing Thoroughbred's neck and urged him to greater speeds. Time seemed to stand still as the big horse ran, the dust spiral drawing closer with each of his magnificent strides.

An old road, barely discernible amidst the grass and sagebrush, appeared beneath Image's hooves and the going became easier. She followed that route, guiding Image around gopher holes in their path. Ahead of them lay an old barbed wire fence and wooden gate. If she took time to open it, she'd miss whatever caused the dust.

As she drew closer, she saw that the top rail of the gate had fallen off, making the obstacle only about three and a half feet high. Heather guided Image toward it and without objection and to her extreme relief, the horse sailed over. They raced on.

Heather heard it now. A truck swerved over the ridge of the hill. She waved her arm and shouted, "Help! Please help me!" Image reared as she pulled him to a stop.

In her excitement she hadn't recognized the pickup, but actually she'd only seen it once before. Her mouth dropped open and for the first time, Dallas's gruff face proved a welcome sight. Better still, from across the cab of the truck Colton said, "Heather! You're covered with blood! Are you all right? Where's Ty and Katie?"

"What the devil's going on?" Dallas asked.

She ignored their questions and shouted, "Follow me, Ty's been hurt." She kicked Image into a canter and started back up the road.

Lather formed on the gelding's neck and his breath came in deep gasps. She reined him in slightly. Again she asked too much.

The truck stuck to Image's heels. When they approached a fence, the horse jumped it. Colton piled out of the truck and opened the gate. Several minutes passed before he and Dallas caught up with them.

Vehicle and horse traveled more carefully now. All sign of a road had vanished and rocks and sagebrush hindered them. Image slowed to a trot and Dallas shifted the truck into four-wheel drive. It seemed to Heather they'd never reach her injured friend.

Finally, after they had climbed one more hill and rounded a bend, they saw Katie hurrying out to meet them. "Heather, thank goodness. Where did you find them?"

"They found me." Heather swung off Image. The horse stood, head down, breathing hard. She wrapped his reins around a tree branch.

The doors of the truck flew open and both men piled out. "We saw Heather's note, but everyone was gone," Colton said.

"Hurry. Ty's over here." Katie motioned.

"What happened to him?" Dallas asked.

As his uncle scooped Ty into his arms and started for the pickup, he stopped deathly still. Dallas's mouth fell open and a look of pure shock registered on his face. "You! What the . . . You're dead," he stammered.

Chuck withered beneath the man's stare.

Little beads of sweat formed on Heather's forehead and her mouth went desert dry. A new spot of crimson had seeped through Ty's shirt. She couldn't stand seeing him this way.

"I'm not who you think," Chuck managed to say.

"This is Chuck, Uncle Dallas, Charlie Phipps's son." Katie stepped between them.

Dallas's lip twitched. "Son, huh? Didn't know he had one." He continued on to the truck and hefted Ty onto the seat.

Colton slid in behind the wheel and leaned over to steady his brother. Dallas opened Ty's shirt, lifted it and examined his nephew's back where the edge of a bloody exposed rib poked through the skin.

Above the pounding in her ears, Heather heard Katie say something about getting Magleby for this. Heather grabbed her friend's arm for support and tried to focus. Too late. She felt herself sink to the ground.

Next thing she knew, Chuck was bending over her.

Dallas joined him. "That settles it." He picked her up and sat her on the seat beside Ty. "You're going with the boys."

Colton turned the key in the ignition. Ty slumped against Heather, his face white as a sun-bleached skull. She tried to swallow and coughed.

"I know this is a ridiculous question," she said, "but what about Image?"

Dallas reached behind her to the gun rack at the back of the cab. "You've got him broke in now. Katie can ride him. He'll travel along fine."

Handing a rifle to Chuck who'd mounted Partner, Dallas said, "You shoot, of course."

The boy glanced up. "I guess . . . uh . . . of course."

As the pickup sped off, Heather glanced over her shoulder. Sitting very straight in the saddle carrying the rifle, Chuck seemed like a different person. Dallas rode beside him on Sage. Katie followed, squirming on Image's English saddle.

Heather hoped the gelding would behave, but no doubt Katie could handle him. The girl was tough. At least she hadn't passed out in front of everybody. Heather felt embarrassed about being so wimpy—guilty too. It should have been Katie sitting here beside Ty, not her.

"What happened back there?" Colton shifted the truck out of four-wheel drive.

Heather skimmed over the events of the last day as quickly as she could. Talking about them made her cold inside and she was so worried about Ty she could scarcely think.

Darting across the dirt road in front of them, a jackrabbit narrowly missed death.

Ty's weight pressed against Heather as Colton barely slowed for a curve.

"How's Dad?" Ty whispered and Heather felt a tinge of shame warm her face at not having asked herself. Even now Ty managed to think of everyone but himself.

"I'm pretty sure he'll be . . . okay," Colton said. The hesitancy with which he spoke made Heather wonder if he weren't holding something back.

Ty hunched forward. Thankfully he'd passed out again. Heather nestled him against her shoulder.

"You care for him a lot, don't you?" Colton said.

Heather tried to talk, but a lump in her throat kept her from answering. Tears trickled down her cheeks.

"Me too," Colton said. After that he kept his eyes riveted on the road while Heather prayed they'd get help in time.

CHAPTER TWENTY

Colton laid on the horn as the pickup screeched into the hospital's parking lot. A white-coated man and woman ran from the emergency exit of the one-story hospital. The building looked more like an elementary school than a medical facility.

"Here?" Heather asked.

"It's small, but good—and close." Colton leaped out of the truck and helped the nurse and aide lower Ty onto the gurney.

Heather slipped from the truck, stumbled and caught herself against the fender.

"You're hurt too," the nurse said. "I'll . . ."

"I'm okay. Help him."

The nurse held up her hand. "I'll be back for you."

They whisked Ty away. Heather followed them into the building and down a long hall until they disappeared behind two swinging doors.

Trudging into what appeared to be a waiting area, Heather collapsed into an overstuffed chair. She glanced around the small but pleasant-looking, carpeted room with a TV tuned to *General Hospital* hanging in one corner. She'd just relax a moment before investigating further. A clock ticking on the wall drew her attention. It read 2:25. Hospitals, at least the ones Heather knew of, usually had people scurrying around pushing wheelchairs and drawing blood. Where was everyone? Would they have someone around who would take good care of Ty?

Elbows on knees, Heather tipped her head into her upturned palms. One hand caught in her hair and she flinched. Blood trickled down her cheek. She wiped the blood away with the tip of her shoulder.

She held her hands in front of her. Dirt and blood crusted her nails and caked her skin. Her jeans were filthy, torn at one knee, and the front of her shirt was stiff with blood. Her wrists, raw and sore where Magleby had tied her, stung when she moved them.

Heather spied a wall phone just outside the room and standing, reached for it. Had Colton already called the police to help Dallas in the search?

"Heather," a voice said, "did you come to see Wells?"

Spinning around, Heather came face to face with Bea Taggert. The woman cocked her head and stared. "What happened? Is that blood?"

"I . . . Ty . . ." Her mind flip-flopped like a trout on land, and her eyes stung with tears.

Bea pulled Heather into her arms. "What is it, dear?"

"I'm so sorry. It's Ty. He's been hurt. Colton's with him in the emergency room."

"Ty's here?" Bea stiffened as she leaned away. "But last night he was . . . what happened? Did one of his horses throw him? Where's Katie?"

"She's okay. Dallas is looking out for her," Heather answered quickly, relieved to have something positive to say. At least she hoped it proved positive. She wasn't about to tell this woman her daughter was on the trail of a murderer. Katie would be safe, Heather promised herself. Dallas would make sure of that.

"I've got to see him." Bea walked briskly to the swinging doors.

"I don't think . . ." Heather started to say.

Colton almost collided with his mother as he returned. "No, Mom." He took her shoulders and turned her around. "You can't go in there. Ty's insides are goofed up and he's lost a lot of blood. They're doing everything they can. We better go talk to Dad."

Feeling like an intruder, Heather hung back.

Bea reached for her. "Come with us, dear."

Heather's throat burned as she tried not to cry. She could be tough as oak when people were mean to her. When they were nice, her strength shredded like cobwebs.

His hand was bandaged to the size of a ham, and an IV dripped into one arm, Wells turned, grinning a feeble greeting. His smile faded as he noted the drawn faces of his wife and son.

"Ty's been hurt," Bea said and sought the comfort of her husband's side.

Struggling to sit, Wells reached for her with his uninjured hand. "Hurt? How bad?" His brow wrinkled.

A doctor appeared in the doorway. "Sorry to bother you, Wells, but I need this consent form signed. Ty's bleeding internally. We're going to have to go in right away."

"He's going to be all right, isn't he, Jack?" Wells's voice sounded strained.

Wells called the doctor by his first name. In Montana everyone seemed to be on a first-name basis.

"I won't lie to you, folks," Dr. Jack said. "I know you like things straight. We won't be able to tell what we're up against until we get inside. We're pumping blood into him now. Bea, you and Colton can see him for a minute before we take him into surgery."

Swinging his leg over the edge of the bed, Wells tried to follow.

"Oh, no you don't," Jack said. "We've almost got you stable, so no messing around. Comprende?" He glanced at Heather.

"I'll make him mind." She ached to see Ty, but knew only family could go.

The doctor's eyes narrowed. "Let me take a quick look at you." He walked to Heather, checked her pulse, studied her face, then parted her hair carefully with his fingers. "Here. Tip your head this way a bit. Ouch! I'll bet that hurts."

"A little." It hurt more than that and she'd just noticed a large bump on her arm, surrounded by scratches. But Ty . . . "Don't worry about me. I'm fine."

"You're stable at least and the cut's stopped bleeding. As soon as I can, I'll get somebody in here for you. Are you feeling okay?"

Heather nodded.

"Good. We'll be back. Bea?"

After squeezing Wells's shoulder, Bea hurried away with Colton and the doctor.

Heather and Wells watched them go. Neither spoke. Then Wells focused on her. "Why don't you tell me what's going on? What happened to Ty? How did you get hurt? Where's Katie?"

She eased into a chair and blew out a long breath. "Ty . . . he . . ." Her voice cracked.

Wells touched her hand, clenched on the armrest of the chair. "Ty's strong and stubborn and he's a fighter. He's gonna be fine." Wells cleared his throat. "He just has to."

Tears stung her eyes. Wells loved Ty, no hiding that. He loved both his sons. Heather knew for sure now. Maybe Wells had sensed Colton slipping away. She rubbed her temples. Was that how it was with her stepfather, Kevin? Did he still love her as much as ever, even though lately his attention had been focused on her new brother? After all, Robby needed Kevin most. She wiped her nose across the back of her hand.

"Won't you tell me what happened?" Wells asked, his voice soft.

How to begin? "Katie's with Dallas. They're chasing Magleby."

"Who?"

"The guy Charlie talked into robbing the bank for him," Heather said.

"The bank? He's not that robber who escaped . . ."

She nodded. "Charlie wouldn't give Magleby his share of the money after the bank robbery, so . . . so Magleby killed him."

"What?" In spite of his injury, Wells straightened. "Magleby killed Charlie?" He shook his head. "How do you know all this? And Katie. What's she doing chasing him?"

Heather opened her mouth to explain, but closed it as Bea and Colton returned to the room. Colton held his arm around his mother. She wiped her eyes with a tissue. "Ty's headed for surgery," she said. "We're to wait here."

Wells fell back against his pillows. Heather stood so Bea could have the chair and moved over by Colton.

"Maybe hearing what Heather just told me will help us wait," Wells said. "Bea . . ." His eyes sought hers. "Heather told me who killed Charlie."

Bea's color faded. "Charlie didn't kill himself?"

He shook his head.

"Who?" She stared wide-eyed at Heather like she was afraid of what the girl might say.

Colton leaned against the wall, folding his arms across his chest. He tipped his head toward Heather as if to say, Well?

Pulling at the neck of her shirt, Heather said. "I guess I better start at the beginning."

"Good plan," Colton said. "And that would be . . .?"

"That would be when I looked for Katie after you all left yesterday and couldn't find her . . . or her horse. It hadn't occurred to me earlier when I'd seen her riding Partner through the fields that she'd been heading in the direction of the shortcut . . ." Heather shook her head. "I think she hoped to find answers. I should have known she'd go there."

"Answers? What shortcut?" Wells asked.

Heather watched for his reaction as she continued, ". . . the shortcut to Charlie's."

He stared at her, mouth twisting, then said. "So, you know about him?"

Nodding, Heather went on. She told about going to Charlie's ranch, seeing Magleby's horrible face staring at her through the window, and how the awful man had caught her.

Sweat dampened her forehead. "Is it hot in here?"

"You better sit down," Colton said, bringing a chair from the other room. "Rest for a while."

"May I have some water?" Heather asked.

"You bet." Bea poured her a drink from Wells's plastic hospital pitcher. "You don't have to tell us any more right now if you don't feel like it. But you're sure Katie's safe?"

Heather handed the glass to Bea. "I'm pretty sure. She and Chuck are with Dallas."

"Chuck?"

"Oh yeah. I need to tell you about Chuck, don't I? He's Charlie's son."

"Charlie had a son?" Wells asked.

"He sure did and . . . does." Heather returned.

"Uncle Dallas thought he was Charlie," Colton said.

"Katie said Chuck looks just like an old picture she'd seen of Charlie." This from Heather.

"What picture?" Wells asked.

"Are you feeling better?" Bea said.

"Sure. I'm fine now." Heather leaned back in her chair and continued with her tale. She told about her night of terror with Chuck, the next morning when Magleby had confronted everyone about the money, and how he'd admitted killing Charlie.

"Magleby killed Charlie?" Colton asked.

Heather nodded and wondered about the strange expression that flashed across his face. "Did you get hold of the . . . the police?" She mouthed the last part.

"They're on their way," he said quietly.

When Heather told of Ty's arrival and the beating he'd suffered, Bea's control evaporated and she sobbed uncontrollably. Heather's voice broke again and she couldn't go on. Wells acted uncertain about how to comfort two women when he felt so bad himself and looked to Colton. The boy's green eyes blazed with rage at what Magleby had done to the brother he'd appeared not to care for. He put his hand on Heather's shoulder. In times past, she'd have welcomed the attention, but not wanting to be disloyal to Ty, she bent away from his gesture, pretending to examine a bruise on her ankle.

"If only I'd have thought about searching the cellar earlier, then maybe Magleby wouldn't have hurt Ty," Heather stammered. "It was only a guess, but it seemed like a place where Charlie might have hidden the money, and Magleby had searched everywhere else."

Heat crawled up her face when Heather spoke of an earlier visit to Charlie's ranch—the time Colton had kissed her—and how she'd seen the cellar after the cow chased her up the tree. She folded her arms across her middle and rocked forward in her chair. Words came more easily when she told about leading Magleby to the cellar, about him finding the money and how she'd trapped him inside.

"I ran back to the house and, I don't know how we did it, but we got Ty onto Partner. Chuck rode behind to steady him. Katie grabbed Ty's horse and slipped out just before Magleby, who'd somehow broken out, shut the gate.

Closing her eyes, Heather brought her fingertips to her brow as her ears began to ring.

"Put your head between your knees," Colton said, hands on her shoulders lowering her down. "I'll get a cold cloth."

He disappeared into the bathroom, bringing back a damp towel. "Hold this to your face."

The coolness cleared her thoughts and she sat up. She wiped around the sore spots on her chin, temple and cheeks and continued on to her hands, cleaning herself up the best she could. She swallowed hard. "Magleby thought he'd trapped me. Actually he had until . . . until Image jumped the fence."

"What? You're kidding," Wells said.

"Yeah. Guess I'm gonna have to be nicer to that horse." For a fleeting moment, Heather's mind switched to another concern. Was it wrong to wonder about Image? Of course she hoped Katie was fine, that the gelding had behaved and that Chuck and Dallas were safe. Yet she couldn't help worrying about her horse. Was he okay? Were his slender Thoroughbred legs still sound? Would Katie know how to care for him when they returned to the ranch? Colic could be a vicious killer when horses weren't cooled down properly after a hard ride.

CHAPTER TWENTY-ONE

You're a brave girl, Heather," Wells said.

"Not really. Maybe none of this would have happened if I'd kept my nose out of everyone's business."

"You're not to blame," Wells said. "You helped bring things into the open that have caused grief for decades." He looked at his wife. "Isn't that right, Bea?"

Shaking her head, she stammered, "I thought Charlie killed himself because of me. I figured I was the last one to see him alive. Right after I told him about Diana—his miserable, low-down, husband-stealing twit of a wife—he turned up dead. All these years, I've felt responsible."

"Twit? Such language coming from my sweet little wife?"

"She was one, you know," Bea returned.

Wells cupped her chin in his good hand.

Heather watched fluid drip from the IV bottle into his arm and wondered what gadgets they had hooked to Ty.

"I saw Charlie after you did," Wells said. "Probably right after Magleby killed him. I should've known you could never hurt anyone. I wasn't thinking straight. You were so upset when you came home that day. You wouldn't tell me where you'd been. I already figured you'd gone to Charlie's because Raymond, remember our hired man, said you'd headed toward there. That's why I went. I was stooped down beside Charlie's body when Dallas came in."

Pondering what she'd just heard, Heather rubbed the back of her neck. She pictured Bea running away from the Phipps Ranch just before Magleby showed up to argue with and kill Charlie. She thought about Wells discovering the body and Dallas showing up. Talk about timing.

Wells grimaced and Bea jumped to her feet to feel his forehead. "I guess Dallas thought I'd killed Charlie," Wells said. "Right away he said we should make it look like suicide."

Heather breathed in the pungent scent of rubbing alcohol and antiseptic. She tried to get comfortable in her chair.

Bea arranged the covers around Wells and stared at the clock, even though Dr. Jack had said there was no way of telling how long Ty's surgery would take.

"I wondered why Dallas would try to protect me," Wells went on, "but I got to thinking afterwards that maybe big brother played some part in Charlie's death. He was the one cow-eyed over Diana. I didn't say anything, though, because I could never sidestep the notion that you might have had something to do with it." His eyes misted as he looked at Bea.

Heather pinched the bridge of her nose. Hmm. Wells must have gone to Charlie's cabin the day of the cattle drive to make sure nothing remained to incriminate Bea, not to protect himself. Heather could only imagine how he must have felt when he saw the blood Chuck had left on the carpet.

Bea's chin trembled. "Dallas wanted Diana? You didn't?" Her voice went hoarse and she touched Wells's shoulder. "Diana told me she was going to take you away from me." Bea swallowed. "She was so pretty. I thought she could do it. I felt there was no way I could hold onto you. That's why I went to Charlie to see if he could help—maybe put a leash on that wife of his."

A leash and a muzzle, Heather wanted to say. Diana certainly got around.

Lowering her head, Bea placed both palms over her eyes. "Charlie laughed. Poked fun at me. Said I couldn't hold onto my man. I was such a fool." She shuddered, dragging her hands down her face. "I slapped him. He yelled at me to get out. I screamed, 'I wish you were dead!' I've never been that mad before."

Her voice squeaked. She cleared her throat. Wells poured her a drink of water. She took a sip then traced the rim of the cup with her finger. "Charlie just grinned. Reached into a drawer and pulled out a gun. 'Here,' he said. I gasped, turned and bolted out the door. He laughed as I ran away." She shook her head slowly. "If the earth would have opened up and swallowed me down, I wouldn't have cared. I couldn't tell anyone, Wells, not even you."

Bea returned to her chair and slumped into it. "When I heard Charlie had killed himself, I felt like I'd pulled the trigger myself. I wondered if finding out Diana wanted to leave him had driven him over the edge."

Wells reached for Bea's hand and held it to his cheek. "I'd never leave you for Diana or anyone. How could you think such a thing? You're my life. Diana meant nothing to me. I told her that over and over." He sighed. "But with Charlie dead, she seemed to think she and I could be together. I told her it wasn't going to happen—to leave me alone. One day I even shoved her. Sorry to say I wasn't much of a gentleman. That's probably why she turned on us so violently, even accused us of murdering Charlie. Luckily, she had no proof."

Husband and wife stared into each other's eyes. Except for the soft beep of the machine monitoring Wells's heartbeat and the rhythmic tick of the clock, the room was silent.

"Anyone in here need sewing up?" Wearing a flannel shirt, jeans and hip waders, a tall man with thinning hair and a sunburned face clomped into the room.

Wells raised his injured hand. "Yeah, me. Hi, Frank."

"Anxious are you? I hear you'll get your turn as soon as the ambulance returns from Butte." He glanced at Heather. "They said it was a young girl. Would that be you?"

"Are you a doctor?" she asked, leaning away.

"You're scaring her, Frank." A nurse followed him into the room.

He scratched his head as if he hadn't really noticed how he'd come dressed. "Oh. Sorry."

"How's the fishing?" Wells asked.

"Always great. All those years in Los Angeles, I didn't know what I was missing. Now that I've got my priorities straight, I fish full-time and doctor on the side." He held out his hand to Heather. "Would you like to wash up before we stitch your head? We've got a shower across the hall. Vera will show you. Then we'll find you something clean to put on."

"Not one of those gowns that hangs open in the back, I hope."

"How about hospital scrubs?" Nurse Vera said.

"Do you have them in lavender?" Heather grinned.

"Only green, that lovely sort of pea soup green. Of course we'll give you some of these cute little blue booties to go with them." She held up her foot to model.

Heather chuckled. "Thanks."

The nurse led her down the hall. They squeezed past two gurneys and three IV poles.

While Heather peeled off her filthy clothes and wrapped herself in a towel, Vera adjusted the water temperature.

In the shower, Heather lifted her chin to let the water run over her face and through her hair. The shampoo stung and she quickly rinsed it off. Blood from her wound mixed with the water running off her body. She turned her sore side away from the spray, discovering more scrapes and bruises on her arms and legs and a large bump on her shoulder.

"Are you okay in there?" Vera stood guard outside. Her voice reminded Heather of Bea's.

Poor Bea. All these years she'd wondered if Wells had loved Diana while Wells feared Bea had killed Charlie. Dallas thought Diana the murderer and Diana wondered which of the Taggert brothers had killed her husband. How weird could it be—a regular whodunit central.

"I'm fine," Heather called. "But how much gunk do you think this drain can handle?"

A few more minutes and she stepped from the shower. She slipped into her own underwear and pulled on the green scrubs and blue booties. She rolled up the pantlegs and pulled the string tight around her waist to keep her britches in place. The bottom of the shirt reached her knees.

Vera gently rubbed Heather's hair and placed a dry towel around her shoulders. She gave her a damp cloth to hold against the bleeding side of her head and led her to a small room.

"Hop up here." Vera patted an examining table.

The doctor, minus his waders, walked in, wearing a white coat over his flannel shirt and jeans. He had blue booties on like Heather's, only his fit better.

She lay on her side, her head on a pillow. "You're not going to shave any of my hair, are you?"

"Don't do that anymore." He parted her locks with his fingers. "Oh yeah. There it is. It's a beauty. Probably take five or six stitches. I'll just clean it up with a little saline and then we'll deaden it a bit. You won't feel a thing."

Vera handed him a syringe.

Heather didn't care how much it hurt. It would be nothing compared to what Ty had gone through. She gritted her teeth.

"Had a run-in with a bad guy, huh?" the doctor said.

"Yeah. Have you heard anything about Ty, the boy we brought in?"

"He's still in surgery. They've paged Dr. Frandsen. He's an oral surgeon. Don't worry. We've got great physicians here." He winked. "Don't let the waders fool you."

She smiled.

"Now let's have a look at those wrists and get you a tetanus shot."

When Heather returned to Wells's room, she heard him say, "Don't wander off, Colton. If there's anything else that needs to be said, let's get it out. There have been far too many secrets left festering."

"When I think of how our lives have been tainted, it makes me ill," Bea said. "If only we'd have just spit it out—not been afraid to talk to each other. Oh hi, Heather. You're back, and looking much better. I was going to ask if anyone knew why Dallas was at Charlie's that day."

It was as if they instinctively kept talking so they wouldn't be forced to discuss how long Ty had been in surgery.

"I asked him that," Wells offered, "but he talked in circles—some silly story about checking the fence line. I think he was probably there to see Diana."

"You're right." Colton walked to the foot of his father's bed. "You're right on both counts. Dallas was there to see Diana and there have been too many secrets—secrets that have given me an excuse to act like a jerk." He studied the floor, then leveled his gaze at his dad. "Dallas hoped Charlie's death would look like suicide because he thought Diana had done it. He was in love with her and he believed she loved him. She was clever enough to play Dallas along for whatever good it could do her even though she loved you, Dad." Colton shook his head. "I don't know, maybe she thought Dallas would be an acceptable second—a consolation prize."

Colton paced the small room. "Dallas didn't realize until later that Diana hadn't killed her husband. But even though he felt like an idiot for letting her use him, he couldn't admit what he'd done to protect her. He was too embarrassed, that and he'd have real explaining to do to the authorities. I suppose that's something we'll have to face now."

"Dallas and I will have to explain. We'll keep everyone else out of it." Wells said.

The hands of the clock continued to mark time. Ty had been in surgery for over three hours. Gnawing pain tore at Heather's stomach.

"I don't know why Uncle Dallas told me this stuff," Colton continued. "I guess he had to tell someone and felt I was the only one he could talk to. A plane's cockpit gets pretty snug on long flights and we're friends as well as family."

Heather frowned. Maybe, or Dallas had used his secret to drive a wedge between Wells and Colton, the son Dallas could never have. She moistened her cracked bottom lip. Be nice. Dallas had been a pretty welcome sight earlier that day.

Colton stopped pacing and peered into his father's gaunt face. "It wasn't until I heard about Magleby that I knew for sure you hadn't killed Charlie. Don't you see, for years I've been living with the dread that my father was a murderer."

CHAPTER TWENTY-TWO

"No!" Heather screamed, and stiffened. Magleby's face, peering out at her from the window, disappeared. Her eyes flew open and she stared at a blank, white ceiling. She brought a hand to her throbbing head and noticed her bandaged wrists. Of course. The hospital. She must have fallen asleep, passed out or something.

Ty? Had the doctor come into Wells's room to tell them Ty had come through the operations, or had she dreamed it? She struggled to her feet, then sat back on the bed to clear her head.

"You're up." Vera, the nurse who'd been so nice the day before, walked into the room. Had it been the day before? What time was it? Where was everyone?

"Yeah, sorta. Is Ty out of surgery? Where's . . ."

"Everyone's gone, except Ty, of course. He's in the recovery room, still unconscious. That's not unusual in cases like his where there's been a head injury." She reached for Heather's wrist, placed her fingers on the pulse and studied at her watch.

"Is he going to be okay?" Heather asked.

"I believe this morning they expect a full recovery." Vera jotted notes on the clipboard she'd carried into the room. "He'll be in the hospital awhile and there'll be recovery time, but he should be good as new."

"And Wells?"

"When the ambulance got back, he and Bea left for Butte. He's been scheduled for reconstructive surgery."

"Do you think they'll be able to fix his thumb?"

"How's our girl today?" Dr. Jack sauntered in, wearing jeans and cowboy boots beneath his white lab coat.

"I'm good. Did I pass out or something? The last thing I remember I was in Wells's room, then I woke up here." Briefly Heather wondered if the doctor planned to go fishing today.

"I gave you something for your headache, don't you remember? Right after I told you about Ty. You fell asleep in the chair. Colton carried you here."

Taking a penlight from his pocket, Dr. Jack shone it into Heather's eyes. "Look over here," he said, leaning close. "Now over here. Good."

"So Ty's gonna be okay?"

"We think so. There was awhile last night he really had us worried, but he's tough—a little wobbly right now, but he'll soon be strong enough to get bucked off one of those broncs he rides."

Heather chuckled. "And Wells?"

Jack glanced at his watch. "He's probably in surgery right now. From what I understand they'll take what's left of his thumb and wrap it in a flap of flesh lifted from his abdomen. One side of the flesh will remain attached to his body until the skin has grown around the bone of the thumb. Then they'll sever the flap from his stomach area, freeing the restored thumb. He'll have to be in a body cast for several months to prevent injury to the operation site."

"Sounds complicated," Heather said, sighing. "So I guess Colton's gone too?"

"Yep," Vera answered. "He left right after his folks did. Said he had something to check into."

"They wanted you to stay here to be with Ty." Dr. Jack winked. "You're okay with that?"

"Yeah." Heather felt heat rise in her cheeks. "When can I see him?"

"Now, if you like, but I want to prepare you. He looks pretty bad. Cuts. Abrasions. His jaw's wired shut. One eye swollen closed. The rib punctured his lung and lacerated his renal artery. Although we took the stomach tube out of his throat, he's got oxygen running into his nose, IV's in both arms and monitors wherever else we could find space to stick them."

Tears filled her eyes as she thought of what he'd gone through . . . for her. "Let's go."

Dr. Jack and Vera walked Heather down the hall, past framed wall photos of the hospital staff.

"Later, if you feel like it, you may want to go out there." Vera motioned toward a glassed, outside door.

Heather looked out on a grassy area with bushes and a wooden bench. Across the road a herd of horses grazed lazily, swishing their tails.

"A lot of our patients like to sit in the sun and watch the animals."

"Looks nice," Heather said.

When they came to Ty's room, she hesitated.

"We'll leave you alone with him, if you want," Dr. Jack said. Then he and Vera disappeared, leaving Heather standing in the doorway.

Ty lay still. The head of his hospital bed raised him up enough for Heather to see his handsome face, now swollen and bruised, the stitched gash below his eye, and the one along his cheekbone. Like Dr. Jack had said, tubes exited Ty's nostrils, continued across his face and hooked behind his ears.

She covered her mouth with her hand and walked into the room. She pulled a chair beside the bed and sat for several minutes, just watching him. She thought of all the fun times they'd shared that summer, the pranks they'd pulled, how he'd helped her with Image and listened to her troubles. She choked back a sob.

"Oh Ty," she whispered. "You were so brave, so very brave." Reaching through the metal slats on the sides of his bed, she touched Ty's wrist above the IV needle.

"I've been so worried," she continued. "We all have. That creep Magleby. He's such a . . ." Katie's word "scumbag" fit nicely. "He's the king of all scumbags."

Standing, Heather paced across the back of the room. Then she returned to Ty's side and lowered herself into the chair. "But they'll get him. Dallas and the sheriff will find him and make him pay for what he did to you."

Vera came in to check Ty's vital signs and made a few notes on the clipboard at the foot of his bed. "You feeling okay?"

"I'm fine. Thanks."

She squeezed Heather's shoulder. "Call if you need anything," she said and scurried out of the room.

With her arm propped on the side of Ty's bed, Heather rested her chin on her hand and listened to his labored breathing, grateful that he was breathing at all. "Look at your poor face, your poor handsome face." She sighed. "You really are handsome, you know. I noticed that right off. That night you came into my room without your shirt, that night I screamed. For a minute when I saw you, I couldn't remember my nightmare."

Ty's knuckles were torn and raw. Somehow talking to him, telling him things she'd never say if he could hear her, helped her cope with what had happened. "I guess I thought Colton was handsome—well, Colton is handsome. You both are, but there's something about you, something that sets you apart." She cocked her head. "What is it, you ask?"

Working things out in her own mind, Heather rambled on. "Let me think. Charisma. Yes. Charisma and . . . sex appeal." Heather rolled her eyes. "A definite yes on the sex appeal, but there's more. I know." She held up one finger. "You're strong, yet vulnerable and kind. That's it."

She sat back in her chair. "Boy, I sound goofy, don't I?" She paused, thinking. "Goofy in love, more like it."

There. She'd said it. She gasped a quick breath. Well, that explained a lot, didn't it? She loved Ty. She knew it now. She must have loved him all through those months she could only think of Colton. He must have been an inner defense against her feelings for Ty. After being hurt so recently by David, she probably hadn't felt safe enough to allow herself to get close to someone else, someone for whom she could care so deeply.

Suddenly an unhappy thought wrinkled her brow. What if Ty just wanted to be friends? She chewed her thumbnail. She'd check things out with Katie. That's what she'd do. Heather swallowed hard. Katie. If only she were back safe and sound. She desperately hoped Colton would have good news when he returned.

After staring at nothing in particular on the wall, Heather glanced back at Ty. His eyes were open—well, one eye, as wide as the swelling would allow. He stared at her.

"Heather. Heather, is that you?" he said in a barely audible voice.

She rested her hand gently on his chest. "I'm here, Ty. You're going to be all right. Don't talk if it hurts."

"Stay with me," Ty struggled to say through swollen lips.

"I'm not going anywhere."

"Closer." Ty's voice sounded raspy.

"What did you say?"

"Come closer."

Heather lowered the metal side of Ty's bed and leaned down against him until her ear brushed his lips.

"Tell me something," Ty mumbled.

"Sure, Ty. What?"

"Did I hear you say you love me?" he asked in a voice as normal as his wired jaw would allow.

Jerking her head back, Heather narrowed her eyes. She thought of all the things she'd said, things she'd never have told him if she'd known he was listening. Her hand stiffened on Ty's chest. "How long have you been awake?"

"You love me, don't you? You can't deny it."

Not even his injuries could shadow the delight in getting one over on her. It was all a joke to him. Embarrassed, Heather leaned away to stand. He grabbed her hand. "I love you, too."

She dropped back into the chair. "Really?"

"Really. I can be charming when . . . not tripping, or acting stupid because I'm . . . ignored." He slurred several words, but spoke remarkably well with swollen lips and wired jaw.

"You are charming." She smiled at him. "And you know it."

Ty's hand moved to the back of her neck, drawing her closer. Their lips touched. "Oh! Ouch!" he said.

Heather kissed him gently on the forehead, the only place on his face that retained a normal color.

"That's more like it," Katie said, bursting through the door. "I've been working overtime to get you two together, but you wouldn't listen. Nobody listens to me." She stopped at the foot of Ty's bed. "You look awful, but they tell me you'll live. Cool. Wish I'd have known that earlier."

All Heather could do was stare while Katie ranted on. "Yes, we got that rodent Magleby, and yes, Image is fine. He dumped me once, but I think it was merely because of that fool saddle of yours." She paused long enough to take a quick breath, then continued. "Isn't anybody glad to see me?"

Standing, Heather gave Katie a huge hug. "Glad to see you? Are you kidding? My stomach feels like its been run through a shredder. Do you have any idea how worried we've been?" She gripped Katie's shoulders and held her at arm's length. "By the way, after everything you've been through, you look great. How come I'm such a softy?"

"Adrenaline, I guess, and I didn't get smacked in the head like you did." She cupped her hand to the side of her mouth. "Actually, aside from worrying about this guy, I've been having a blast."

"You have?" Heather cocked her head. "What happened after we left?"

"It was so cool. I felt like a regular vigilante. There we were, riding along on our horses, rifles in hand. Well, I didn't have a rifle, but I was riding along . . . well, . . . until Image shied—uh

bolted at a jackrabbit and dumped me, but anyway . . . Uncle
Dallas legged me back on that dinosaur you call a horse and we
rode off, neck 'n'neck, kinda like the Magnificent Seven."

Katie's blue eyes gleamed. "We got back to Charlie's, turned
the horses into the corral, and sneaked into the house. We
searched all the rooms. It was weird seeing where we'd been. I
showed Uncle Dallas where Magleby tied me up and he got
kinda teary-eyed and put his arm around me. I never thought he
liked me much. Poking through Charlie's house could've been
real creepy if Dallas hadn't been there. No sign of Magleby,
though. We searched the outbuildings and the barn, even the
cellar where you'd locked him in."

Scooting her chair next to Ty, Katie lay her hand on his arm.
She nodded toward him and smiled. He'd fallen asleep again. "I
have that effect on men."

Both girls giggled.

"Then what happened?" Heather asked.

"Chuck got the idea to check where he'd left his old truck. We
figured Magleby would be looking for transportation since he'd
probably hitchhiked or walked to Charlie's. Uncle Dallas said
he'd wondered about that old truck sitting alongside the road
since the last time he'd come through."

Why hadn't she seen it? Heather rubbed the back of her neck,
then remembered she'd always taken the mountainous route to
Charlie's.

"We mounted up and off we went, the Magnificent Three on
the trail again," Katie continued. "When we got to where Chuck
left his truck, I couldn't believe it. There he was—a big monster
out of a nightmare. At first he didn't see us because he was
fiddling with the motor."

Katie twisted the end of her braid around her finger. "Then he raised up so quick he bumped his head on the underside of the hood. He grabbed the pillowcase he carried the money in and lit out for . . . for . . . well, anywhere but there. He moved pretty fast for a big man, but, of course, he was no match for the horses. We were on him in seconds. Uncle Dallas made a lasso and let it fly. What a sight. It settled right around Magleby's shoulders and jerked him off his feet. Ty's horse kept the rope tight while Uncle Dallas piled off and ran toward Magleby. That scumbag struggled to his feet trying to loosen the loop around him. I reached for my lariat, but your saddle can't carry one. I yelled at Chuck to throw me my rope, but he had the shotgun aimed and Uncle Dallas had already bulldogged Magleby to the ground, kneed him in the back and tied up his hands. I half expected my uncle to throw his arms in the air and ask how many seconds he'd taken."

Heather yawned.

Katie pulled a face.

"I'm sorry. Can't seem to get my pep back," Heather said, dropping into her chair. "Go on, though, tell me everything."

Gently touching Ty's swollen jaw, Katie frowned. "We made that creep walk all the way to Charlie's. I got to carry the money. Magleby kept saying he was sorry, that he didn't mean to hurt Ruby. He's more than a few cards short of a deck, I think. Sheriff Dan and his deputy got there pretty quick and hauled him off in the back of their Blazer. They'd have come back to take us home, but we had the horses to look after and all."

"I feel bad. I'll bet Image was a pain," Heather said.

"Actually, by that time he was pert near tolerable." Katie rolled her eyes and continued. "We took the shortcut across the mountains to the Buck Place. We got home real late last night, put all three horses in the barn and fed them a nice alfalfa dinner. Image was still laying down when I checked him this morning, only jumped up to nip Sage over the side of the stall."

"Sounds like he's no worse for wear. What about you?" Heather slid her chair closer to Ty. "Magleby treated you kinda rough too, Katie. Are you okay? Here I've been relaxing in the hospital while you and Chuck have been traipsing all over the territory and I'm the one's who's so tired I can hardly wiggle. Has the doctor had a look at you? And what about Chuck? Where's he?"

"Dr. Jack's been chasing me around with a stethoscope." Slapping her knees, Katie stood and paced to the opposite side of Ty's bed. "They want to run a few tests, so I guess they'll be coming for me soon. It's crazy. I feel great. Chuck's with Uncle Dallas. They'll be here before long. They're thicker than two pups from the same litter. I wouldn't be surprised to see Chuck stick around for a while. Like this morning, those two were visiting so much, I couldn't get them moving." She studied the machine monitoring Ty's vital signs. "Colton said he'd bring me in to see Ty. Of course I had to promise to let the doc have a look at me."

Slumping forward, Heather lay her head down on the side of Ty's bed. "I'll just rest my eyes for a minute."

She thought she heard Colton say, "No, let her be. It'll make Ty heal faster than anything the doctor could prescribe." Katie said something, then Heather heard another female voice, probably Vera's.

The last thing Heather remembered was that the back of her head rested against the side of Ty's warm body and his hand lay on her shoulder.

CHAPTER TWENTY-THREE

Heather sniffed, dashed away a tear, and peeked through the poles of the old corral. Maybe watching the horses would make her feel better.

"Hi, boy," she said, as Image trotted by—neck bowed, tail flowing. "You're kinda pretty these days." Although she'd never thought him overly handsome before, nearly three months of ranch work had transformed him. A layer of muscle covered his once protruding ribs while his belly sucked up wasp-like.

"But you're beautiful," she told Lady Roxanna, the mare Ty had shown her weeks ago during their trip to Beaver Springs. The golden-red coat of Ty's dream horse contrasted sharply with Image's brown black. Heather thought of a porcelain sculpture as mare and gelding frolicked in the dawn of the new morning.

Strong arms circled Heather's shoulders as Ty came up behind her, holding her close against his lean body. He rested his chin on the top of her head. Even after a week in the hospital and another recuperating at home, he seemed to have lost little of his strength, though he still walked slightly bent and his jaw would be wired shut for another ten days. Living on soup and milk shakes, he was eight pounds lighter but vowed to gain them back when he could "wrap his teeth around a beefsteak."

Heather turned in Ty's arms. Clinging to him, she willed time to stop so she could stay with him forever. She wished she were eager to see her family again. Once she would have been—before they'd grown tired of her. She was excited to see her favorite horse, Possum, and yeah, probably her family . . . a little. But thoughts of leaving Ty, the rest of the Taggerts, and the addictive charm of Montana made her feel like her soul was being yanked out. She'd tried to put off returning home for a little while longer, but the clock had worked against her. College started soon and the state fair was only two weeks away. Her folks planned on arriving today to take her and Image back to Utah.

"I don't want to go." Heather tipped her head to look at Ty and felt tears clinging to her lashes. It didn't help that he wore the hat she'd helped pick out.

"I'm not too crazy about it either," Ty mumbled, then cupped her face in his hands and kissed her.

Side by side, they watched the horses. "Looks like Roxie's going to miss Image too," he said, draping his arm around her shoulders, "but not nearly as much as I'm going to miss you."

"I can't even think about it," Heather choked out through the tightness in her throat. "I know how bad Roxie's going to feel. Hmm. I'll be with her boyfriend and she'll be with mine."

"Me?" He raised a questioning brow and grinned. "I like that—you calling me your boyfriend." He sighed and stared skyward. "I don't know if Roxie can take your place or not."

"Better be not." She nudged him in the side with her elbow. "Say, you're getting pretty good at talking with your mouth wired shut."

He drew her closer. "If I don't make it as a vet, maybe I can be a ventriloquist."

Heather had no doubt he'd make it. Ty would be a wonderful animal doctor someday. "How about a vet ventriloquist? You could have the animals tell you what's wrong with them."

"Good idea." He squeezed her shoulder. "Look at that mare. Isn't she something? And she's mine. How did you ever talk Dad into buying her, let alone putting up part of the money?"

Image and Roxie stood head to tail, hind legs cocked, swishing flies off one another.

"It wasn't that hard really. I visited him at the hospital in Butte. We had a nice chat." Heather chuckled. "The cast around his arm and middle was driving him crazy. He had a bent-up hanger in his good hand that he kept poking down inside to scratch the itches. We talked about you for a while and he scratched. Then we discussed my stepfather, Kevin, and our horses and he scratched some more. When I told him what a beautiful horse I thought Roxie was, I asked him if he wanted me to work the hanger on his back where he couldn't reach. About the time I suggested Roxie would be an excellent investment, he'd have agreed to anything."

Ty laughed.

A magpie landed on one of the corral's fence posts, squawked a couple of times, then paused to watch them. Another black and white bird joined the first and they debated in loud cackles.

"Kinda reminds me of Katie." Ty went cross-eyed.

Heather hid a smile behind her hand. "Be nice," she said and cleared her throat. "Actually, I wish I could take more credit for your dad, but I can't. I think after seeing how much Magleby hurt you, he'd already decided that if you made it, he'd help you get a horse worthy of you. You should've seen how upset he was when we brought you into the hospital. Besides, he only had to put up half the money. The other half was yours."

"Because you gave it to me," Ty said.

"Not really. It was as much yours as mine."

Heather thought of the five thousand dollar reward for recovery of the stolen bank money that at first she'd wanted to turn down. She was glad now she'd told the bank people to divide it four ways, with Ty, Katie, Chuck and herself each receiving equal portions.

"It was your share, fair and square, and if you'd have used my twelve hundred and fifty dollars, your dad wouldn't have had to pay a thing."

Ty rubbed the side of his nose. "Oh yeah, sure—take all your money. I already feel guilty enough. You'll need it for college."

"I'll manage. Besides it's found money. I didn't plan on it. Actually, though, I think your dad wanted to put up the money."

"Do you? Having you and Dad involved makes Roxie even more important." He shook his head and laughed. "You and Katie really had me going last Monday—out of the hospital two days and you guys drag me out to the barn at night. I thought you were going to dump water on my head or something."

"We'd never do a thing like that," Heather teased.

"Oh no. Never." Ty shook his head.

"Did you have any idea?" Heather asked.

"You kidding me? If I'd have known Roxie was in our barn, I'd have dragged you guys out there."

Heather laughed. "I thought it was a stroke of pure genius on Katie's part to tell you that Dallas bought your dad a new cow pony for one hundred and fifty dollars. She knew you'd have to see that horse for yourself."

"Dang sneaky. It took me a minute to register that it was Roxie in the stall and another several to realize she was mine." He drew Heather into a hug. "How will I ever repay you?"

"I'll think of something."

The mare sauntered to them, stretching her long neck over the top pole to nuzzle Ty's palm. Much to Heather's surprise, Image followed and stood beside the sorrel.

"Do you want to ride her?"

"Really? I thought you'd want to be the first," Heather said.

"I'd like to see you two together."

"Okay. She's broke, isn't she?"

"You bet."

Snatching halters from a corral fence post, they caught both horses. The magpies, apparently weary of watching, took to the air.

The barn smelled of alfalfa, leather and cedar shavings. Heather noticed a lariat hanging on a peg and took a quick breath. The last time she'd seen a rope in this barn was when it had sailed through the air and caught Katie. She remembered Ty's smiling face and how she'd thought he looked like a big kid. She wished now she'd savored every minute they'd shared. Struggling to swallow, Heather turned Image into a stall.

Ty bridled and saddled Roxie, using his well-worn tack. The mare stood quietly while he shortened the stirrups.

Image paced the confines of his stall, and when Ty led Roxie out to the corral again, the gelding pawed and whinnied.

Though he didn't need to, Ty held Roxie while Heather put a toe into one stirrup and swung her other leg over. She wiggled around in the Western saddle, stood in the stirrups, sat, and wiggled some more.

"Something wrong?"

"No. This is a comfortable saddle," Heather said.

"You should try one of your own again. Remember that day with the sheep? A few more months in Montana and I'd have you completely converted."

Roxie's long stride was smooth as waves on the rolling sea. Heather cantered her around and around the corral.

"I don't know who's more beautiful, you or Roxie," Ty said, when Heather reined the mare to a stop.

"I'll take that as a compliment," she said.

"It was meant to be," Ty said.

Image's neigh sounded from the barn. Roxie stared longingly in that direction.

"Isn't it funny," Heather said, smoothing the mare's mane. "Image is usually such a beast with other horses, even at first with Partner, but he liked Roxie right away."

"He's got good taste . . . like me." Ty grinned up at her.

She smiled. Off in the distance she watched a big puffy cloud form in the deep blue sky—the same sky she'd stare at and think of Ty when she got home.

How could she bear to be four hundred miles away? "What am I going to do without you?"

"Just keep missing me. Don't fall for some city boy."

For an instant Heather wondered if she'd ever mentioned David, her boyfriend of last year. Well, Ty had nothing to worry about. "No one can measure up to you," she said.

"Don't you forget it." He wagged a finger at her.

Roxie's ears flipped back and forth as Ty and Heather talked.

"That goes both ways." Heather studied the stitching on the bridle reins. "I've seen some pretty good-looking chicks while I've been here."

"Really?" Ty said. "Rhode Island Reds or Bantams?"

"Don't joke. This is serious." She swung down from Roxie, landing close to Ty. He took her into his arms.

"This is a sad, sad day, isn't it?" Katie said, approaching from the house.

Heather and Ty jumped away from each other.

"At ease," Katie said, grinning. "Don't mind me."

Heather smiled at her friend. There was something different about her today. Usually she seemed much younger than her fifteen years, but today, dressed in a bulky western shirt she'd undoubtedly swiped from Ty, she seemed closer to Heather's age of two years older. Maybe it was that her kinky red hair cascaded down her back instead of being twisted into its usual braids, or perhaps it was the way Katie carried herself—straighter, more confident.

"It is a sad day," Ty said.

"Super sad," Heather said. "I wish it were June again."

"This time we'd hogtie Colton," Katie said. She secured a strand of hair behind her ear. "He still flirts with you, doesn't he?"

"Oh, flirting comes so natural to him it's like breathing. He knows . . . he knows . . ."

"Yes . . .?" Ty tipped his head toward her.

"He knows . . . you're my guy." Heather touched his shoulder.

Katie folded her arms across her middle. "What you gonna do without me to supervise your romance?"

"I don't know," Heather said. "Do you supervise long distance?"

"Believe me, she'll try," Ty said.

Roxie pulled on the reins Heather held in one hand. Ty took the mare and tied her to the fence.

"Just make sure he writes, okay?" The thought flashed through Heather's mind. David hadn't written.

"You can count on me." Katie ran her fingers through the hair. "And we'll get to see you if you testify at Magleby's murder trial."

"That's right." Heather had almost forgotten about that. She still had nightmares about their ordeal with the murderer. Katie said she never did. In fact, the redhead told the story with gusto to any unsuspecting listener, embellishing it whenever possible. "And the blood was spurting out of Ty. We didn't think we'd ever get it stopped." Now that Magleby was back in jail and the new charges and better security would probably keep him there for life, everyone's stress level had lessened.

"I'll use any excuse I can to come back." She smiled at Ty, who moved to stand at her side. "Speaking of trials, the law and stuff, will Dallas and your Dad have to explain about Charlie's death— I mean about making it look like a suicide?"

"Oh, didn't I tell you? That's all taken care of." Katie lifted her hair from her neck, retrieved an elastic band from her pants pocket, stretching it around her curls to form a high ponytail. "Uncle Dallas talked to Sheriff Clegg the other day. Dallas didn't go into much detail but said something about statute of limitations and 'letting sleeping dogs lie.' You know, he didn't even mention Dad was involved. He told the sheriff he'd done everything to protect Diana."

"I'm liking your uncle more all the time," Heather said.

"Me too. Know what else happened?" Katie asked.

"What?" Heather said.

Ty glanced at his watch.

"In town the other day, Chuck saw those guys who stole our calves—you know the ones he ran into at Charlie's? He and Dallas followed them home and got the calves back. Of course the babies didn't look real good. The kids had them on milk cows—didn't agree with them, I guess. Dallas threatened to bring charges. He didn't, though—just wanted to scare the boys. He was probably so relieved that the law had gone easy on him, he felt generous. Oh, he told them that since the calves had gone down so much in value, Chuck was keeping the fifty dollars they gave him to keep quiet."

"Sounds like Dallas and Chuck are pretty thick," Heather said.

"It does, doesn't it?" Katie said.

"Is Colton all right with that?"

"He seems okay," Katie said. "But haven't you noticed? Colton's been with Dad a lot more than usual."

"I've noticed." Ty said. "Actually with both Dad and me out of commission, he's been a lot of help. You both have too. You know, come to think of it, I wouldn't be surprised if Dallas asked Chuck to stay."

"That reminds me." Katie wiggled between Ty and Heather, placing an arm around each. "Chuck just radioed from the home ranch. Your mom called there. She's not coming to get you because your baby brother's sick, but your stepfather stayed in Idaho Falls last night and will get here later this morning. She said to tell you to be ready."

"I'll never be ready," Heather said, more to herself than to the others.

"I wish you didn't have to go." Katie's eyes watered. She blinked several times and forced a smile. "Now I'm gonna have to put up with Ty's moping. It'll be the pits."

"My mom's gonna have to put up with me."

"Why don't you just marry her, Ty?" Katie asked. "Then she could stay here."

Ty coughed and started to laugh. Heather felt her face color. "That's a thought," he said. "Maybe we'll discuss it sometime when we're alone." He took Katie by the shoulders, turned her toward the house and slapped her on the backside like he would a horse.

"Okay, if I leave, will you discuss it now?"

Ty squinted his eyes at her.

"No one else will bother you either," Katie said over her shoulder. "Dad and Mom are headed to Butte to check on Dad's thumb and Mr. Flirt, I mean Colton, has gone to town for supplies. So you're alone—all by yourselves."

Image whinnied from the barn. Roxie answered.

"Ain't love grand?" Katie said, grinning.

"Good-bye, Katie," Ty said.

"Good-bye, Ty," Katie answered in a low voice, mimicking his. She turned and strolled to the house, her ponytail swinging as she walked.

Ty faced Heather, taking her hand. He rubbed his thumb across the knuckle of her ring finger. "If there should come a time when I'd ask you . . . you know . . . what Katie suggested, how would you answer?"

Heather studied the buttons on the front of his plaid shirt, then peered directly into his liquid brown eyes. "I'd have to say . . . I'd say YES."

Grinning, Ty lifted his hat and wiped his forehead with the back of his sleeve. "I needed to hear that before I let you go."

CHAPTER TWENTY-FOUR

Image's hooves sounded against the boards of the old barn and his whinny sent the sparrows perched on the rafters into flight.

Ty and Heather looked at each other. She shook her head. He shrugged. They both laughed.

"Do you think he'll be ready for your big shindig?" Ty asked. "I'll set the jumps if you want to work him."

It had been so much fun last Wednesday when she and Katie gathered barrels, poles, old gates, sagebrush and any loose ends they could carry and designed a jumping course. "I thought you were collecting junk for the dump," the recuperating Ty had said, causing Katie to break into giggles. Soon all three were holding their stomachs, laughing.

Just thinking about it now made Heather chuckle. "No. I'll set the jumps," she said. "You're still an invalid—remember?"

"And here you are—planning to leave me in my moment of need."

"I'm a heartless creature, and you, with your mouth still wired shut, your poor face all beat up . . ." Heather touched his cheek. Actually, his face looked good—really good. The deep purple bruises had paled to a medium brown and the scars on his cheekbone and chin had lightened to thin red lines. The swelling was completely gone. Her own injuries had all but disappeared when the doctor removed the stitches in her scalp several days earlier.

Ty winked. "What do you think? Will I be able to go out in public any time soon?"

"Yeah. OH YEAH." Swaying, Heather put a hand to her heart in a mock swoon.

After spending almost the entire summer in jeans, this morning she had dressed in riding boots and breeches, for Kevin's sake, and she'd packed the rest of her stuff.

"Invalid! Hey. It takes more than a little operation to keep a good man down. Here, let me do that." With ease, Ty grabbed a pole Heather had hardly been able to lift.

"Okay for you," she said. "You remind me of your dad's saying: 'When it's true, it ain't bragging.'"

"Darn right." Ty rolled a barrel into place.

Within minutes they'd set up the entire course. Ty walked to Roxie, untying her. Heather followed them into the barn. Image greeted the mare with enthusiastic nickers.

"I'll unsaddle her," Ty said. "And after I give her some grain, I'll take her back out so when you jump Image he'll behave— maybe."

Image's saddle lay across the side panel of a stall, the bridle over it. Heather slipped the newly oiled headstall over the gelding's ears and placed the English saddle upon his sleek back—a final time before leaving Montana. She thought of the kidding she'd taken many times during the summer because of her chosen saddle and smiled.

They waited for Roxie to finish her grain before leaving the barn.

After securing the mare outside the corral, Ty stood in the center of the hastily constructed jumping course. "Okay, let's see if he learned anything at summer camp."

The big black's neck came up and he pranced around the corral. Heather urged him into a canter and circled several times before heading toward the first jump. Like the champion Kevin hoped Image would become, the gelding sailed over a pile of sagebrush supported by poles on barrel ends. They leaped the six remaining jumps. Perfect. Heather's smile grew wide. She reversed him and took all seven jumps in the opposite direction. The horse she'd brought to Montana three months ago—the horse she'd feared—no longer existed.

She glanced at Ty. He gave her a thumbs-up. He'd told her she could train Image and with his help, she'd done it. Kevin would be impressed.

A tingle shot up her spine as she thought of what they'd accomplished. She and Ty had worked hard, Image too. He was a pretty nice horse—not as sweet as her own Possum, but saving her life had definitely earned him points. She had to admit she loved the old devil.

"Good job, Heather. You've worked wonders with him," Ty shouted.

"I agree," said another voice.

Reining Image to a stop, Heather stiffened. The voice belonged to her stepfather, Kevin.

The dark-haired man and Katie walked toward them. "He's still cute," the girl mouthed and fanned herself with her hand.

Yeah, Kevin was cute all right, and more—movie star handsome, built like an athlete, always dressed as if he'd stepped out of a catalog—and he loved animals, especially horses, especially Possum. In fact, the man's interest in her horse had been instrumental in bringing Kevin into Heather's family. Once they'd all been so close, but she doubted he'd even missed her this summer.

"I'm Kevin Quinn," he said, offering his hand. "You're Ty? I've heard a lot about you."

"Don't believe it." Ty returned the handshake.

"Thank you for looking out for Heather. How are you doing now?"

"I'll soon be good as new. Should be getting these wires off in a week or so." Ty rubbed his jaw.

"That's the spirit. Hard to keep a good man down," Kevin said.

Ty chuckled. "That's just what I told Heather."

"Great minds, huh?"

"Yeah." They laughed.

Heather's mouth twisted. Kevin got along with everyone lately, except her. Once she'd been important in his life. Now he considered her a burden, someone to get out of the way, someone to send to Montana so she wouldn't interfere with his new family. How was she supposed to act? He hadn't even told her hello.

She slid off Image. Ty stepped to her side and slipped an arm around her shoulder. "You remember Heather, don't you?"

"Heather." Kevin tipped his head.

Katie scowled.

"What do you think of the horse? Looks good, doesn't he?" Ty said.

"He does, remarkably so." Kevin ran his hand along the black's neck. "What's your secret?"

Ty smiled. "Heather did it."

Katie shinnied up the fence and perched there, watching. "She's a wonderful rider and trainer."

"She's a wonderful girl." The stare of Kevin's intense blue eyes fell on Heather.

Her heart thumped wildly. She took a step forward. Her mind whirled. Did he really think she was wonderful? Ty looked from one to the other. Katie shifted her position. A cow mooed in the distance.

Then something happened that surprised Heather. Kevin held out his arms.

With Image trailing behind, she slipped into her stepfather's embrace. His arms closed around her. Tears trickled down her cheeks.

"It hasn't been the same without you," Kevin said. "It's time you came home."

"You want me to?" Heather backed up to stand beside Image. "I thought you were glad to be rid of me."

"How could we ever be that? I thought it was the other way around—you wanting to get away from us."

"I didn't want to get away. What made you think I did?"

"Don't you remember how distant you were? How you'd go out and spend evenings in the stable with Possum instead of doing things with the family?" He dug in the dirt with the toe of his spit-polished oxfords. "That time we all went to the movie—even took Robby—you said you'd rather stay home."

"I'd already seen it and I had to study." She frowned. Actually she'd been waiting for David to call. He hadn't.

Heather glanced at Ty who flashed a quick grin. Katie sat on the fence, speechless for once.

"And then," Kevin gestured with an upturned palm, "you acted like you preferred to train Image by yourself—didn't want my help."

She pressed a hand to her temple. Everything Kevin said was true. She had avoided them—felt they no longer needed her. They had Robby, their child together. She was a different combination; someone else's daughter. She looked at Ty again and thought about everything he did for his family. What had she done for hers? Had she offered them anything? Had she tried to be Robby's big sister?

As if Kevin had heard her thoughts, he said, "And then there's Robby. Aren't you glad you have a little brother?"

"Of course I am." She squared her shoulders. "I love Robby. I just don't know anything about babies. I was afraid I'd hurt him."

"You won't hurt him," Kevin said, his eyes moist.

How could she have been such a spoiled rotten, childish, self-centered brat? She lowered her head. And such a weakling? She was afraid of being around Robby, and when riding Image had scared her, she'd given up. She hadn't wanted Kevin to see what a bad rider she was. Anyone could handle Possum. "I thought you wanted me to train Image, no matter what happened to me."

Reaching out, Kevin cupped her chin in his palm. "I hoped you'd train Image. I wanted you to learn to trust one another. Not so much because of what it would do for him, or me—but what it would do for you. You seemed to have lost faith in yourself." His eyes narrowed. "Believe me, it was hard to let you go, but you needed a victory. Image is a tough horse, but I knew you were up to the challenge."

He touched her cheek where a slight bruise still showed. "I had no idea what other challenges there'd be. When your mom and I heard about that murderer, we wanted to rush right up and get you, but remember, you wouldn't agree to it." He rested his hand on her arm. "If anything ever happened to you, I don't know what we'd do, and now you don't even want to go home."

"It's not that I don't want to go home, it's that I don't want to leave Montana."

"Or someone in Montana?" He nodded toward Ty.

Heather rubbed her hand down Image's nose. "Something like that."

Kevin stood erect like he was going to deliver a speech. "Maybe I can help. I've already discussed this with Wells and Bea, and if Ty gets everything cleared with the doctor, his parents say he and Katie, if she wants to, can come down and watch you at the fair. That is, if you're still planning on competing."

Heather threw her arms around Kevin. "Oh, thank you. Thank you. Ty, Katie, do you think you can?"

Ty cocked his head. "Sounds fun. We'll have to see if we can get away."

"Sure we can." Katie clapped her hands and barely saved herself from tumbling off the fence.

"See, I'm not such a bad guy." Kevin glanced down at Image's legs.

"I never said you were a bad guy." She watched as he stooped to feel the gelding's fetlocks. Heather held her breath for fear he would discover some unsoundness in Image she'd overlooked.

Standing, he continued. "Think about how things looked to your mother and me."

Heather chewed her bottom lip. "I'd have kicked me out too."

Kevin threw his hands in the air. "I didn't kick you out. I arranged for you to have a new experience in a beautiful place. Actually, you owe me a lot."

"More than you know." She smiled at Ty.

"And now I'm going to have to take you away. In fact, we'd better get loaded."

"Can't you at least stay until Mom and Dad get back?" Katie jumped from the fence. "They really wanted to see you. And Heather, you haven't had a chance to say good-bye."

"I know, but somehow I can't face telling them good-bye."

Kevin took Image's reins from Heather. "I'd love to stay, but there's a little matter of a horse show in how many days, Heather?" He studied her and she shrugged. ". . . and then there's college, and Heather's brother is sick and her mother is all alone. I'm sorry, but we have to get back. If we leave right away, we can make it home before dark."

* * *

As Heather hauled her stuff to Kevin's truck, she felt as if she walked in a trance. Her legs moved but her mind wouldn't focus.

"Need help?" Ty asked.

"Absolutely not," she said. "You know you'll overdo again."

Katie had disappeared, leaving Heather with the impression that her red-haired friend didn't like good-byes any more than she did.

Lingering in the doorway her last trip in, Heather tried to memorize each detail of the room that had been hers—the brass bed, the round, oak-framed mirror above the old chest of drawers, the woven rugs on the hardwood floor. Her stomach ached and she could hardly swallow. She would miss Ty so much. She would miss everyone and everything in Montana. She felt as if she'd never be whole again.

Ty came up behind her. "I have something for you," he said. "Sort of a going-away present."

"But I didn't get you anything."

"This was last minute. Here, put your suitcase down, turn around and close your eyes."

Heather did as she was told. She sensed his arms pass in front of her face before he secured something around her neck.

"There. Come over here and look in the mirror." He took her hand.

A silver key hung suspended on a matching chain around her neck. The key reminded her of the kind used to open doors in old English mansions, only smaller. David had given her a necklace too, a running horse on a chain, just before he went away to college. She hoped this wasn't a sign of things to come.

"It's beautiful, Ty. Thank you. Is it a key to your heart?" She batted her eyes.

"You could say that," he returned.

"You have my heart too." She hugged him. "Leaving's so hard. I didn't know it could hurt so bad."

"I know," he said and held her tighter.

They stood a moment, unable to let each other go. Then Ty said, "Well, this will never get any easier."

"I know, and maybe you'll come to Utah for the fair. That's not very long."

"We'll keep telling ourselves that, anyway." Ty reached for her luggage.

Heather glared at him and handed him a much lighter sack. "Good-bye room," she said and started down the hall.

* * *

Kevin had removed Image's saddle and wrapped the gelding's legs for travel. Ty glanced at Heather with an our-horses-never-get-that-kind-of treatment look and she smiled.

"About ready?" Kevin asked.

"As ready as I'm gonna get," Heather said.

Roxie whinnied as Kevin loaded Image into the trailer. Ty walked to the fence where he'd tied her.

"That's a beautiful mare, Ty. You wouldn't want to sell her, would you?" Kevin asked.

"She's pretty special." He grinned at Heather. "Maybe her colt in a few years, but it'd be expensive. Roxie's the beginning of my new herd."

"Good choice. Quarter Horse or Thoroughbred?"

"Registered Quarter, but plenty of Thoroughbred early in her pedigree."

Kevin nodded.

Still hesitant to make the final move and get into Kevin's truck, Heather stood outside with Ty. Kevin slid behind the wheel. It seemed he didn't know what to say any more than Heather or Ty.

"Hold on a second," Katie said, as she came from the house. "We have something for you."

She handed Heather a gray kitten. "Smoky wanted you to take Ringo home so you won't forget us."

Heather had managed to keep a rein on her feelings until then, but as she took the kitten from Katie, she burst into tears. Ty wrapped her and the kitten in his arms. Katie put her arms around all of them.

After squeezes and pats, the three drew away from each other. Still Heather couldn't force herself to climb into the truck.

"Here, Katie." Ty handed her the cat. "Hold Ringo a minute."

He placed his hand on the side of Heather's neck, beneath her hair. "It's gonna be a while before I can do this again, so with your permission, sir . . ." He nodded at Kevin. "I'd like to give my girl a proper good-bye kiss."

"If you have her permission, you have mine. I say go for it."

"I'll hold the cat," Katie said.

Talk about center stage. "Here? Now? In front of everyone?" Heather felt her face flush.

"You bet." Ty's hands rested on the sides of her jaw. He tipped her face up and smiled into it. With one finger he brushed aside a tear that rested on her cheekbone. His lips parted and he bent closer. "I love you, Heather," he whispered.

"I love you too," Heather said quietly and told herself to breathe.

His lips, soft and gentle, touched hers. His hands dropped to her shoulders and he pulled her close. She smelled the hung-out-on-the-line-to-dry scent of his shirt. His mouth, more demanding now, seemed hesitant to ever leave hers. Behind closed eyes, she pictured neon lights flashing and lightning bolts across a dark sky. He'd kissed her before, but never like this. When he drew away, her lips followed his and he gave her another quick kiss, then pulled her into a hug.

"Wow!" Katie exclaimed. "On a scale of one to ten, ten being best, I'd say that was a definite fifteen."

"Not bad for a fellow with a wired-shut jaw," Kevin said. "Are you going to be someone I'm going to have to worry about when you're all better?"

"I hope so," Ty returned.

"Hmm. Maybe it's good we're leaving."

"Oh, he's harmless," Katie said. "Now Colton . . . But we won't discuss him."

"Let's not," Ty said. He opened the door of the truck for Heather and she climbed in. Her throat felt even tighter.

"Good-bye," Katie said.

Ty tipped his head and touched the brim of his hat.

"Mind if I don't say good-bye?" Heather said. "I'll see you— like in two weeks."

Katie handed Heather the kitten.

"See ya," Heather said as Ty closed the door. She cuddled Ringo close to her face and, taking hold of the kitten's front leg, helped him wave to his former owners.

Both Ty and Katie laughed, then returned the gesture.

It wasn't until they were several miles down the winding dirt road that Kevin spoke. "If things work out between you and Ty, do you think he'll give me a good deal on that colt?" His eyes twinkled.

Tears rolled down Heather's cheeks, but she managed a smile. Her hand settled in the softness of Ringo's fur.

During the next several hours, Kevin kidded with her and asked her opinion on important horse issues, really listening for her response. She couldn't remember him ever being so attentive.

Before she realized how far they'd traveled, she sighted the big, blue, green and white "Welcome to Idaho" sign in the distance. She turned in her seat for a final backward glance. "Good-bye big sky. Good-bye mountains. Good-bye beautiful, beautiful state." She drew a long, unsteady breath.

"How ya holding up?" Kevin asked.

Heather stroked the kitten, who woke from a nap on her lap. "If we stop and let Ringo 'rest' at the next rest stop, I'll probably be fine," she said, and for the first time that morning she really meant it. After all, her mother, brother and Possum waited for her at home, and she and Kevin were good friends again. Image was ready for the state fair and wouldn't it be something if Ty and Katie could see her ride?

Things were pretty favorable in Heather's world—a world she felt certain would always contain Ty.

About the Author

Sunrise and Me

While growing up, Betty imagined that as an adult she'd either be *Perry Mason's* secretary, a horse trainer, or a writer and illustrator of children's books. Her profession of twenty-eight years—working as a legal secretary—has allowed her to support her horse habit. Creating books has given her the opportunity to combine her love of horses, writing, and illustration into one art form. She lives with her husband, Scott, in Mapleton, Utah. She proudly claims two grown children, four grandchildren and two horses. She is the author of *A Tuff-to-Beat Christmas* and *Quality Concealed.*

Coming soon from Sunrise Selections:

Join Heather, Royal Image, and Possum on the shores of Flathead Lake in northwestern Montana in *Challenge of Choice*, the third volume of the *Heather* trilogy. David and Ty meet and the life of a horse is put at risk.